"I thought the _____ be a good t_____ our partners___

Her eyes gre___

"If you'll ag____ ___ to dissolve our partnership ___ the house, we can get the renovators back to work on the place."

That sounded reasonable, though she wasn't ready to admit it. Her demand to dissolve their partnership had been a knee-jerk reaction on her part. "What will happen when the work is done?" she asked.

"We'll sell the house at a tidy profit, end the partnership and walk away with a nice chunk of change in our pockets."

She considered it for several seconds. It meant living right across the hall from him for several months. She had to ask herself if she could resist the temptation he offered. She looked at his tousled black hair, the slant of his gray eyes, the fullness of his lower lip that could kiss so devastatingly. She *could* handle the temptation.

And pigs could fly....

Dear Reader,

People frequently ask me where I get ideas for my books and I always say that good ideas come from everywhere, but the truth is I'm an unrepentant thief. I listen to stories other people tell me and adapt them for my books. I warn my friends and family not to tell me anything they don't want to turn up in a book some day. After a warning like that, it's amazing that anyone speaks to me.

I've picked up a number of good ideas from all the jobs I've held. Besides being a wife and the mother of four, I've taught school, worked as a librarian and as a secretary, and operated a care home for developmentally disabled children. My favourite occupation, though, is writing romances in which the characters get into challenging situations and then work their way out. Each situation and set of characters is different, so sometimes the finished book is as much a surprise to me as it is to the reader.

Patricia Knoll

Recent titles by the same author:

BACHELOR COWBOY
RESOLUTION: MARRIAGE

MEANT FOR YOU

BY
PATRICIA KNOLL

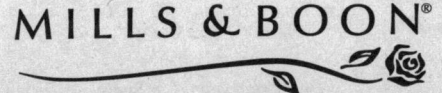

DID YOU PURCHASE THIS BOOK WITHOUT A COVER?

If you did, you should be aware it is **stolen property** as it was reported *unsold and destroyed* by a retailer. Neither the author nor the publisher has received any payment for this book.

All the characters in this book have no existence outside the imagination of the author, and have no relation whatsoever to anyone bearing the same name or names. They are not even distantly inspired by any individual known or unknown to the author, and all the incidents are pure invention.

All Rights Reserved including the right of reproduction in whole or in part in any form. This edition is published by arrangement with Harlequin Enterprises II B.V. The text of this publication or any part thereof may not be reproduced or transmitted in any form or by any means, electronic or mechanical, including photocopying, recording, storage in an information retrieval system, or otherwise, without the written permission of the publisher.

This book is sold subject to the condition that it shall not, by way of trade or otherwise, be lent, resold, hired out or otherwise circulated without the prior consent of the publisher in any form of binding or cover other than that in which it is published and without a similar condition including this condition being imposed on the subsequent purchaser.

MILLS & BOON and MILLS & BOON with the Rose Device are registered trademarks of the publisher.

First published in Great Britain 1999
Harlequin Mills & Boon Limited,
Eton House, 18-24 Paradise Road, Richmond, Surrey TW9 1SR

© Patricia Knoll 1999

ISBN 0 263 81940 X

Set in Times Roman 10½ on 12 pt.
02-0002-51459 C1

Printed and bound in Spain
by Litografia Rosés, S.A., Barcelona

1

"NOT AGAIN! PLEASE DON'T let this be happening again." Caitlin Beck jiggled the key to her apartment door, easing the knob the tiniest little bit to the left, then back to the right as she twisted the key in the lock. When that didn't work, she reversed the process. Still, the door remained stubbornly locked.

"I asked Mr. Mellin to fix this," she muttered, frowning in concentration as she tried again. Frustrated, she thumped her fist against the doorjamb. Of all days for this to happen—yet again—this would be the one.

Murphy's Law in full force.

Caitlin set down her briefcase, balancing it against the soggy bags of groceries she'd hauled up two flights of steps to her door. On top, she stacked the envelopes she'd taken from her mailbox in the downstairs foyer. She crouched down to examine the lock. There was nothing to do but call the building's handyman who was *supposed* to help her out. The trick was to locate him.

Of course, she could step across the hall to her neighbor, but that would bring her more help, advice and information than she needed. She would much rather go into downtown Crystal Cove and search the taverns until she found Barney Mellin, the maintenance man she had hired to help her out until she had full ownership of this building. It was a beautiful, Adam-style Georgian house that had been converted into four apartments—which she intended to convert back into a single-family dwelling. There were any number of young professionals looking for housing in Crystal Cove. This would make an excellent home for a family once the renovations were done. Of course, work couldn't resume until she was rid of the tenant across the hall.

The bottom two floors, scattered with stacks of tile and lumber, rolls of wallpaper and cans of paint, were a mess. She hated passing by it every day, regretted the time being lost, but no further work could be done until the legal problems were settled. And who knew when that would be?

Caitlin cast a dark glance at the closed door behind her, then went back to working with the lock, trying to coax it into opening.

She knew that her affection and attachment for this building were totally out of proportion to its beauty and worth, but she'd fallen in love with it the minute she had seen it standing on a cliff above Crystal Cove, its white-pillared front angled to catch the rays of the setting sun.

Sunset, she had discovered, was the best time to view it because the twilight masked its crumbling condition. She had taken the apartment before she'd had a good look at the place.

How could she have guessed that the stairs creaked as if they were going to collapse any second, the roof leaked and the hot water came from the shower in a pitiful trickle?

It probably wouldn't have mattered if she *had* known, she admitted with a sigh. She'd been besotted, and not only with the house and the small apartment tucked up under the wide-gabled roof directly across the hall from—

"Anything wrong, Caitlin?"

She remained in her crouched position for a minute as

she ran through a few choice words and tried to convince her heart to quit trying to choke her. She would have given almost anything not to have her body experiencing these wild physical reactions whenever she heard Jed Bishop's voice. There was absolutely no reason for it, but they wouldn't stop. Why did Jed always show up at the worst possible moment, anyway? He seemed to have a sixth sense where she was concerned.

"Caitlin? Is something wrong?" he asked again.

She straightened and turned around. Putting her hands behind her, she rocked up onto her toes and gave him a carefree smile. "No, Jed. Nothing at all."

"It *looks* like something's wrong."

Her breezy smile slipped a notch. "I can handle it."

His gaze traveled over her. "You're all wet."

Her eyes widened, her mouth dropped open in mock surprise and she stared down at her suit. "No kidding."

He ignored her smarty-pants theatrics and his thumb flicked out. "Doorknob stuck again, is it?"

"What makes you think that?" She pushed her damp hair out of her face with a nonchalant gesture as she shielded the door with her body. She hated this—being caught in an awkward situation, looking her worst. The rain had soaked her as she left her office. She'd stopped for groceries and received another drenching as she dashed into the market. Then, when her car wouldn't start, she'd stood in the downpour while a passerby had unsuccessfully tried to get it going.

The new hairdo she'd paid a small fortune for only the week before was no longer fluffed and perky. Instead, her chestnut hair was plastered to her head in some places and sticking up at wild angles in others. Her cream linen suit with its wide, sweeping skirt would have to go straight to the dry cleaners, as would her fuchsia silk blouse. She'd left for work looking professional and pulled together and returned home looking as if she'd been dragged backward through a knothole. An underwater knothole.

Her gaze skimmed over Jed. He, on the other hand, always looked good, even dressed in worn jeans and a long-sleeved T-shirt of charcoal gray. And, darn it, she wished she wouldn't notice. His black hair was carelessly tousled as if he'd pulled off one shirt and pulled on another and hadn't bothered to smooth his hair.

She knew exactly how he did it, too. Instead of grasping the T-shirt hem with crossed hands and pulling it over his head, he reached behind his neck and yanked it straight up and off, which meant the necks of most of his T-shirts were stretched out, and... Damn! Peeved, she looked away. She had to stop this.

He had been leaning against the door frame of his apartment. Now he sauntered forward, a knowing grin crooking one side of his mouth, his gray eyes full of wise-guy laughter. "I don't know, Caitlin. Maybe it's because you've dumped your stuff all over the hallway and I'm sure I distinctly heard some very colorful language coming from your ruby-red lips."

"Not until you showed up," she said sweetly, stretching those ruby-red lips into a patently fake smile. "And if you'd stay away, you wouldn't hear anything from me at all."

He shook his head. "Tut, tut, tut. I see we still have to work on our neighborliness—please note that I'm using the word 'our' in the loosest possible way. As far as I'm concerned, *my* neighborliness is just fine, while yours leaves something—"

"How about we don't get into that right now? If you

don't think I'm a good neighbor, you can always move out," she suggested. "My feelings won't be hurt."

"But you'll be lonely," he said, his voice dripping with sympathy. "And I would hate for that to happen."

"Loneliness isn't necessarily a bad thing, Jed, especially when the alternative is having you right across the hall from me."

Again that grin flickered devilishly and his voice dropped to a sexy rumble. "There's a third alternative. You could move in with me. I've got the larger apartment, big bedroom, big bed—"

"Big ideas," Caitlin broke in brightly. "But no thank you. You can continue to sleep in that big bed all by yourself."

He raised an eyebrow at her.

"At least without me," she added.

Why was it that *now* was the time she decided to get so smart? She should have wised up about three weeks ago, kept her goals in mind, discreetly sought information about Jed in Crystal Cove, paid attention to the battalion of women marching through his apartment day and night. She had never seen anything like it. Maria Rossi brought him fresh-baked goods from her family's bakery. Sandra Hudson showed up with curtains she'd sewn for his bedroom, as well as a bottle of champagne and two glasses. Raeann Forbes was writing a novel in which Jed appeared to have a starring role. Two elderly ladies, the Carlton twins, trotted up the stairs to bring him jars of jam and pairs of knitted slippers. There were so many others who sashayed in and out of his apartment that Caitlin had lost count.

Jed greeted them all with delight, inviting them inside. Caitlin tried not to notice how long the young, attractive ones like Maria, Sandra and Raeann stayed, but truthfully, she didn't think it was long enough for them to be indulging in anything illicit.

After all, she knew firsthand that Jed liked to take his time when making love. He said it was something that shouldn't be rushed, and... Damn! She gave herself a mental kick. Besides, it was none of her business if he had relationships going with three women at once, illicit or not.

She was *not* going to remember what it had been like to be in that big bedroom and big bed—at least not for the eleventh time today. She had made a bargain with herself that she would only think about it ten times a day and once she reached that limit, she wouldn't think about it again. Next week she was going to try for five times a day. Eventually the memory would fade away completely.

She was very organized and determined, which was why she was good at her job as an investment counselor and had achieved so much in the four years since college.

Her intelligence and determination had brought her this far. Unfortunately her intelligence had taken a leave of absence a few weeks ago, right around the time she had met Jed Bishop, but she had a grip on her determination that rivaled a first-time sky diver's grasp on his parachute's ripcord.

She pushed her damp hair out of her eyes and braced herself for further persuasions from him, but he gave her a knowing look and changed the subject.

"I've been home for an hour. Where have you been?"

"Working, Jed. It's an activity many people indulge in every day."

"And are they better off for it?" he asked smartly. "That's what I'd like to know."

"Most people think they're better off. It beats being hungry and homeless."

She'd tried to keep her tone light, but it must have betrayed something, because he gave her a swift look.

Caitlin kept her expression pleasantly neutral, hoping he would think it was a casual remark. She didn't really think she had fooled him, but he didn't pursue it. Instead, he said, "I work, Caitlin, only I don't work at the same job every day. I like variety."

There was no denying that. Some days he worked on his land-development deals or checked on the properties he owned around town; other days he drove a truck for his brother's trucking firm or coached basketball at a local youth club. Mostly he spent his time enjoying life.

That was another reason the women in town were so crazy about him. He had a devil-may-care attitude, a killer grin and an easy way of moving that suggested he could change direction at any second and would be happy to carry the nearest woman along in whatever direction he chose. It wasn't so much that he was the town bad-boy type, but more the why-don't-you-and-I-be-bad-together type. It was a combination compelling enough to attract most women. Including her.

He strolled across the hall, took the key from her hand and slipped it into the lock. Of course, it turned right away. Still bent at the waist, he pushed the door open with a touch of his finger, picked up her mail and her grocery bags and, with a deep bow, waved her inside.

Rolling her eyes, she grabbed her briefcase and marched into her living room, which was bright and enticing with its white walls, lushly upholstered sofa and chairs accented by fat primary print cushions, and healthy green plants. The decor was centered around a wall-hung Texas Star patterned quilt she'd bought at a craft fair last year.

She also had a number of found art objects on display.

She loved turning old things into lovely and functional items. She had taken a section of a garden gate, attached a mirror and surrounded it with silk flowers. Her tab-top curtains were hung from coils of electrician's tubing twisted into whimsical shapes above the windows. Her kitchen utensils rested in a can that had once held Italian plum tomatoes. These imaginative touches were at odds with the no-nonsense attitude she projected at work, but she didn't care. She could relax here because it was her home. At least for now.

Relieved to be in her apartment, she turned to Jed. "Thanks for your help," she said briskly. "I'll see you later."

Again that devil's grin flashed. "You know, that's a nice little dismissive tone you've got going for you there. I think I'll pretend I didn't hear it." He glanced around. "Don't I get some kind of reward for opening your door?"

"Obviously I loosened up the lock before you tried it," she said, dropping her briefcase and purse on the antique desk she'd refinished.

"Oh, obviously," Jed agreed, not even bothering to hide his grin.

Caitlin plucked the mail from his hand and took a moment to leaf through it.

Jed carried her grocery bags into the kitchen area and began unloading them.

"Make yourself right at home, Bishop," she said as she flipped through the mail, which she saw was mostly junk. She'd only lived in Crystal Cove a few months. How did all these sweepstakes and lottery entries track her down so quickly?

"Thanks, I will. Anything interesting in the mail?" he asked idly.

She gave him a look that would have had most people backing off. "Not that it's any of your business, but no."

"No love letters from some heartbroken boyfriend in San Francisco?"

She ignored him.

"Considering your line of work, I have to guess that any boyfriends you left there aren't the type to be heartbroken. Too busy watching the bottom line and counting their assets," Jed speculated.

"Jed, I'm not going to discuss anyone from San Francisco with you," Caitlin answered sharply.

To her irritation, he chuckled. "Fine. We'll leave everyone else out and talk about you."

"No."

"Caitlin, I've known you for nearly two months now—"

"Far too long, in my opinion."

"—and I've come to realize that you're not a woman who likes to take chances."

She couldn't argue with that, so she said nothing.

Jed stored some jars of pasta sauce in the cupboard and snapped it shut, then stood watching her with his hands on his hips. He lifted his chin, pointing it at the envelopes she still held. "You should fill out some of those sweepstakes entries and send them in. See what happens."

"I know what will happen. I'll get more. They follow me wherever I go." She tossed them down on the desk. "I'm convinced there are no real organizations anywhere that send these things out. I think these envelopes get together in some mailbox somewhere and breed like rabbits."

Jed's laughter rumbled across the room. "Why, Caitlin, that's the first vaguely bawdy remark I've ever heard you make."

"What can I say? You bring out the worst in me."

"You're damned cute when you say things like that."

Caitlin growled. It was impossible to insult him. Such comments rolled right off him and then he used them as ammunition to toss right back at her. And darn it, why did she have to fight the urge to smile at some of his comebacks?

"Seriously, Cait," he went on. "Why don't you take a chance on even one of those sweepstakes? You never know what luck might bring you."

"I believe in hard work, not luck." Caitlin cringed at her own prim tone. Good grief, when had she begun to sound so stuffy? That was an easy one to answer. When she had met Jed and he'd begun to railroad her into his way of thinking. Sounding stuffy seemed to be a way to establish a line of defense and maintain her independence.

"Then you're missing out on an awful lot in life."

"And you're just the person to tell me what to do to put some spice into my life, right?"

"Spice and sizzle," he confirmed.

The sizzle supplied by him, no doubt. She wished that didn't sound so appealing. "Did anyone ever mention that you've got a bad habit of arranging people's lives for them?"

Jed tilted his head back and pressed his lips together in a frown as he considered the ceiling. "Yeah. Bob Bailey mentioned that to me a year or so ago when I suggested he quit his job at his dad's auto body shop and move to the Cayman Islands."

In spite of herself, Caitlin was fascinated. "What happened?"

"After he told me to mind my own business, he did it. Bought a bar there, married one of the waitresses..." Jed paused and gave her an oblique glance.

"And?" she prompted, curious about why he was avoiding her eyes.

"And a hurricane blew in and wiped the bar off the face of the map."

Caitlin threw up her hands. "I rest my case."

"It was still the right thing for him to do," Jed insisted. "He hated working for his dad." He grabbed a bottle of beer which he had left in her refrigerator on his last uninvited visit and twisted off the cap. He examined the cans of diet cola in the door. "Anything I can get for you?"

"Out?" she asked wistfully.

He slapped the refrigerator door shut and gave her a friendly grin. "You know, if I wasn't such a secure guy, you might make me begin to think you don't want me around."

"I don't want you around."

She ignored the voice calling her a liar and told herself that she hadn't injured his feelings, that it was impossible to do so, but she saw some emotion flicker in his eyes and feared she had hurt him.

He didn't answer. Instead, he took a long, slow swallow of his beer and stared at her for several seconds, the color of his eyes going deep gray. She tried to imagine what he was thinking. It was easier for her if she thought of Jed as a mistake she'd made, then she didn't have to deal with the depth of her own distress because she'd slept with him without really knowing him. Something she had *never* done before. And worse, she was the latest of many women who had fallen for him.

But like it or not, she owed him. He had urged his elderly aunt Geneva to hire Caitlin as her financial adviser. Even though his aunt was on an extended vacation in Los Angeles, she had done so, calling Caitlin frequently for information and advice, for which she promptly paid a substantial fee. Those fees were helping to keep Caitlin's business afloat, and her talks with Geneva Bishop kept Caitlin's spirits up. Geneva was the kind of feisty, independent old lady that Caitlin intended to be. Best of all, Geneva had recommended Caitlin to several of her friends.

Looking at Jed now, Caitlin only seemed able to recall that his initial intervention had helped her start her business.

She knew her soft heart was going to get her into real trouble someday—if it hadn't already. She cleared her throat. "I didn't mean that quite like it sounded."

His eyes narrowed a bit. "Yes, you did. You want me to get out, but you never mention the alternative. You could sell me your half of the building and move out."

"Not if you offered me ten times its value," she answered in a testy voice. "Not now. Not ever."

With a shrug, Jed strolled into the living-room area. "Then we're stuck, aren't we?"

He sat down on her wicker couch, seeming to shrink it to the size of Barbie-doll furniture, and stretched his long legs before him. "I love the way you use words, Caitlin. It must come in handy in your work. Puts a man in his place."

"My words never put you in your place, which is across the hall, by the way."

"I guess I'm immune." He took another long drink of beer. "We're at an impasse over this house, Caitlin."

"Only because you're so stubborn."

"I'm not the stubborn one. Listen, we both want the same thing for this house, this whole project. There's no reason to dissolve our partnership."

"There's *every* reason."

Jed's jaw clenched. "When you get that blue-norther

tone in your voice, I know it's time to change the subject, but this isn't the end of the discussion." He paused as if mentally shifting gears, then said, "How was your day?"

Caitlin slowly released her breath through her teeth. "Fine, thank you."

"Liar. You're wet through and you look like a cat that someone tried to bathe."

Whereas *he,* with his feet stretched out halfway across her living room and his beer bottle resting on his flat stomach, looked like an advertisement for some pop psychologist's relaxation technique.

"If my appearance offends you, why don't you leave so I can change clothes?"

He wiggled his eyebrows at her lecherously. "Honey, you can change clothes while I'm here. It won't bother me at all."

"It will bother *me!*"

"You look plenty bothered already." Jed sat up and focused on her. "What's wrong, besides getting caught in the rain? If it's something to do with our partnership, I have the right to know. What happened?"

Why did she bother to fight it? Even as she asked herself the question, she struggled on. "Our soon-to-be-dissolved partnership," she stated firmly, but he only smiled. With a sigh, she said, "Nothing bad happened at work."

In fact, she'd had a good day, finally managing to convince Mrs. Harbel to put her money in some investments that would give her more financial independence and security over the next few years. She longed to share this little victory with someone. With Jed. But she already knew that telling him might tempt her into sharing further intimacies. She had learned that she needed to keep such information to herself. Unfortunately she had a hard time remembering that when she was around Jed.

She lifted her hand nonchalantly. "Everything's fine."

"Well, then, what is it?"

She growled her exasperation. "If you must know, my car wouldn't start after I stopped at MacAllen's Market. It's still there. One of the cashiers who was getting off work gave me a ride home."

Jed shot to his feet. He could move fast when he wanted to. "Why didn't you say so? Change into some dry clothes and we'll go get it."

"That isn't necessary, Jed. I'm sure it's nothing but a dead battery. The one that's in there is five years old. I'll call Charlie's garage and get it replaced tomorrow. I'll stop by there on my way to work, and—"

"Someone might steal it overnight."

Caitlin hooted with laughter. "My car? A thief would have to be pretty desperate to try making off with it."

"Why take that chance? You never know when a thief might come along and—"

"And what?" she asked. "Have a fetish for a twelve-year-old Nissan station wagon with mismatched fenders and a door that won't open?"

Jed's grin turned slyly reminiscent. "Maybe. Charlotte Ferris used to have a Nissan like that when we were in high school, and most of the guys in town—"

"Never mind," she interrupted.

She wished she didn't sound so prudish, but thinking of him with Charlotte Ferris, a tall, gorgeous blonde with approximately nine miles of beautifully toned legs made her feel a rush of something she refused to identify as jealousy.

"I've offered to lend you money to buy a new car, and

think how much more successful you would look tooling around town in a BMW or a Mercedes.''

This was an old argument. Caitlin held up her hand. ''And have my clients thinking I'm so extravagant I can't handle my own money much less theirs? No thanks. I don't want your help, Jed. I know it's important to look successful and driving a nice car is part of that image, but I want to do this on my own. When I can afford it, I'll get a new car.''

The corners of his mouth pulled down. ''*Now* who's being stubborn? Go change your clothes. We'll get your car.''

With an irate look, Caitlin turned away, entering her bedroom and closing the door carefully so she wouldn't be tempted to slam it. She might be stubborn, but if so, she'd been taking recent lessons from a master.

Her shoulders slumped as she stood by the door, not even cheered as she usually was by the sight of her high double bed with its brass frame and white eyelet comforter, and the fluffy white flokati rug on the smooth golden-maple floor. She loved this room, especially because of the ocean view, but today the sky, the water, everything outside was gray—reflecting her mood.

It had all seemed so simple, she thought morosely as she removed her damp clothes and hung them over the shower-curtain rod in the bathroom.

Since long before she had graduated from college, she had worked and saved every penny she possibly could from her job at the bank so that someday she could open her own office, be her own boss. She had made a careful study of the towns on the northern California coast. Her intention had been to find herself a hometown, one where she could settle and stay settled for the rest of her life, one where she could be part of the community.

Never again would she have to accompany someone who was skipping town one jump ahead of the law, nor would she awaken with a jolt, wondering where she was—what town or city, what room in which fleabag hotel.

Crystal Cove had seemed perfect. It was only an hour north of San Francisco, large enough to have many flourishing businesses and an influx of retirees and young professionals who could use financial advice from a hotshot young investment counselor named Caitlin Beck. At the same time, it had been small enough to possess the sort of friendly atmosphere she liked.

Who could have guessed Jed Bishop would come strolling into her office not long after she opened it, flashing that pirate's grin, appreciating her with his knowing eyes and melting her bones as soon as she reached out to shake his hand?

Who could have guessed that his request for information would lead to dinner, to numerous dinners, movies, dates, to a partnership in renovating this house, to moving in across the hall for the purpose of supervising the renovations, to a celebratory bottle of champagne?

To bed?

Who could have guessed that she, who weighed *every* decision carefully, would get herself into such a mess in such a short time?

Her distress wasn't only due to having slept with someone she didn't really know and love. It was because afterward she feared he saw her as one of his projects, like converting these apartments back into a single-family house, coaching basketball, helping people.

All those things were worthy, wonderful projects, but she didn't want to be one of them. She knew he saw her as a puzzle he needed to solve, but she didn't want to be solved. She wanted... She didn't know what she wanted.

All the women who visited him seemed to be wild about him, and he treated them with warm friendliness, greeted them with hugs and kisses. Why hadn't she *noticed* that he treated her the same way? That to him, she was just one of the crowd, only closer?

Because she had been besotted.

With a grimace, Caitlin jerked open her closet door and grabbed some clothes. It took her only a few minutes to change into a pair of slacks and a blue cable-knit sweater to ward off the September evening's chill. She combed her hair, and because it was a mess, hid it under a San Francisco Giants cap. Grabbing her raincoat, she left her apartment and met Jed in the hallway.

He gave her a quick glance as if approving her warm attire and the new color in her cheeks. Spying the cap, he frowned. "If you hadn't cut all your hair off, you wouldn't have to hide it under that cap."

"Thank you, Jed," she answered sassily. "You always know how to make a girl feel special. If you're going to get my car started, hadn't we better leave now?"

He gave her a disgruntled look, but took her arm and accompanied her down to the sweeping, pockmarked driveway where he'd parked his golden-yellow Mustang. The garage out back was falling down, so neither of them used it.

Caitlin was grateful to see that the rain had stopped, though she didn't expect to see the sun. The clouds sulked on the horizon.

Once they were seated in Jed's car, he reminded her to fasten her seat belt and they took off with a roar.

Caitlin had ridden with Jed before so she knew what to expect. She braced herself against the dashboard, but the turn from the driveway onto the pavement was made on two wheels at warp speed. The force plastered her against the door, and as she struggled upward and gasped for air, she said, "That giant sucking sound you hear is me peeling my face off the window. Can't you slow down?"

He grinned as he flashed her a glance. "What's the point of driving a sports car if you're not going to use all this speed and power?"

"A long life?" she suggested, grabbing the armrest to avoid catapulting into his lap as he took another curve. "Jed, you're a terrible driver."

He gave her a dry look. "Oh, please stop, Caitlin. These showers of praise are embarrassing."

Caitlin turned her face to the window as she bit her lip. Darn him. He was making her laugh again, charming her, exactly as he charmed every female.

The tires shrieked as they reached the town limits. He slowed to a crawl as they passed through a school zone and eased into MacAllen's parking lot. He cruised to a stop and Caitlin worked her fingernails out of the padded dashboard. They left little half-moon shapes behind. "Thanks for the flight," she gasped.

"Anytime."

"Yeah, anytime I want to know what my maximum heart rate is."

"Think of it as aerobics without all that annoying sweat," he advised as he unfolded himself from the Mustang and held out his hand for her car key. "Come on, let's take a look at your car."

"It's a dead battery, Jed. All we have to do is open the hood and—"

"I'll check and make sure."

Of course he would. Exasperated, Caitlin handed over the keys.

Jed tried the engine and was met with nothing but a grinding sound. He cranked it a couple of times, listening carefully. "Must be the battery," he observed, tilting his head in thought. Caitlin wanted to hit him.

"I'll get my jumper cables," he said. "Then we'll see if we can start it."

Caitlin would have offered to help, but he seemed to want to do it himself. She moved away and stood watching the early-evening shoppers stopping for last-minute necessities as she had done. She held the door for a petite elderly woman who emerged from the market pulling a two-wheeled wire cart on which her groceries were loaded.

She glanced up at Caitlin, who was struck by the woman's direct gaze and clear blue eyes. "Thank you, my dear," she said, stopping for a few seconds to look searchingly into Caitlin's face.

Caitlin was about to speak, but something in the woman's expression stopped her. She had an odd little triangular face, hardly lined although she was stooped with age. Her hair was snow white and thick, curling around her face. Her startling bright eyes studied Caitlin for a few more seconds taking on a vague, faraway expression, then she seemed to focus again and she said, "Hello. I was beginning to wonder when I would see you."

The warmth in her soft, quavery voice made the statement sound as if they had met before, were, in fact, close acquaintances.

Caitlin stared, trying to place the woman, but failed. In her work, she had met a number of older women in town, but she didn't remember this one. Deciding the woman was a bit addled, Caitlin smiled kindly and said, "It's nice to see you again, too."

Immediately the woman straightened and blinked at her. "What do you mean, again? We've never met before." With a shake of her head, she moved through the door.

Taken aback, Caitlin released the door to let it slide quietly shut while she gazed after her. Her first response was to laugh, but instead, she shivered. Strange. She felt as if the old woman had seen right into her soul.

Caitlin watched her as she made her way across the sidewalk, carefully avoiding cracks, even lifting her little cart over them. Smiling, Caitlin recalled the old saying "Step on a crack, break your mother's back." This woman seemed to be a strict believer in that, though Caitlin couldn't imagine that the elderly woman's mother was still alive. After several minutes of avoiding the tiny fissures in the sidewalk, the woman reached the curb, stepping off first, then turning to pull the cart onto the crosswalk. One of the bags shifted, and she stopped to set it right. Then she seemed to spy something in the gutter and bent to retrieve it.

Caitlin straightened in alarm when she heard a car approaching. The swish of tires on wet pavement told her it was going much too fast for these conditions. Quickly she glanced around and saw it speeding down the street, its blinker indicating the driver was going to turn at the corner where the old woman was wrestling with her cart.

"Wait!" Caitlin shouted, starting forward. Jed dropped the jumper cables onto the engine and spun around to see what was happening.

Automatically he reached out a hand to her, but Caitlin dashed past him. Grabbing the cart, she shoved it aside and wrapped her arms around the woman, pulling her onto the curb. An instant later she felt Jed's arms close around them both and he dragged them back as the car swept past. It sent up an arc of water, drenching all three of them.

2

"WHAT THE....? DAMN," Jed sputtered. With one hand, he swiped water from his face. "Fool driver."

Caitlin gasped in outrage over the drenching they had taken. "Of all the rude...!" Looking down, she realized she was clutching the woman they'd rescued and Jed was still holding them both. Automatically she loosened her hold on the woman, but stayed close, lightly touching her arm in case she needed steadying. She shifted away from Jed and spoke to the woman. "Are you all right, ma'am?"

The woman brushed water from her face and flipped drops of it from her curly hair. As she shook out the front of her long black raincoat and stomped water from her old-fashioned high-top rain boots, she treated her rescuers to a rueful look. "Well, I'm as wet as a codfish, but I'll survive." Her words were hearty, but her voice wavered. She cleared her throat. "I wonder if my groceries did. I'll be very put out if my fresh bread is ruined."

She started for the curb, but Jed strode ahead of her. "I'll get it, ma'am." He grasped the handle of her little cart and pulled it to safety, then peeked into the bags and said, "Everything looks okay. I guess it's a good thing you answered 'plastic' when they asked."

"Oh, yes, plastic," the woman said. "It's astonishing what they can do with that now. So much more versatile than cellophane."

Caitlin and Jed exchanged puzzled glances. "Yes, ma'am," he said.

Suddenly she gave Jed a sparkling look from her bright blue eyes. "Such polite language. What is your name, young man?"

"Jed Bishop."

She nodded slowly and a smile of recognition spread across her face. "Bishop, of course. Your parents have raised a true gentleman. I knew they would."

Jed gave her a quick scrutiny. "I don't think we've met. Do you know my parents?"

"My name's Reenie. Reenie Starr, and don't be ridiculous. Of course I don't know your parents. I just arrived here."

His eyes darkened in confusion. "Well, then, I don't understand what you mean."

"That's all right," she said, patting his arm. "You don't need to."

Jed glanced at Caitlin again, who smothered a laugh. She recalled the comment Reenie had made while Caitlin had held the door for her, saying she'd been wondering when she would "see" Caitlin. The woman's mind seemed to be wandering.

"I don't?" Jed began, but Reenie veered off to another topic.

"Well, that was lucky," she said. "You were here at exactly the right moment." She glanced up. "It's working already," she said in a tone of pleased wonder.

"What's working?" Caitlin asked, still wiping dirty water from her face. If she'd known she was going to get wet all over again, she never would have changed out of her suit and put on clean clothes.

"The luck, of course." She opened her palm and showed them a shiny object. "'See a penny, pick it up, all the day you'll have good luck,'" she quoted in a singsong voice.

Jed and Caitlin looked at what the woman held in her hand, then glanced at each other. Jed cleared his throat. "Excuse me, ma'am..."

"Reenie," she supplied pertly.

"Reenie," he said. "That's not a penny. It's a copper-colored beer-bottle cap."

She squinted at the item, then dug in her pocket. She pulled out a pair of glasses, popped them on and frowned through the thick lenses. "Well, I'll be darned. You're right." Perplexed, she shook her head. "My eyesight's not what it used to be, but squashed flat like this it looks exactly like a penny."

"And picking it up nearly got you flattened in the street," Jed said.

"Uh, Jed," Caitlin warned, fearing his pointed language would offend the lady. "Ma'am...Reenie. You really shouldn't have lingered in the street like that."

"Well, how was I to know the speed limit had been raised to such an outrageous number? Thirty-five miles an hour. Why, that's appalling." She blinked suddenly, gazing at the stop sign. "No wonder the driver didn't stop. Some trickster has painted that stop sign red, instead of yellow. Someone should speak to the city council about that."

"Yellow stop sign?" Caitlin asked.

"Ma'am, stop signs haven't been yellow since the nineteen fifties," Jed told her.

Reenie glared at him. "I knew that," she said with a firm nod. She shook her finger at him and frowned. "I know what you're thinking."

His eyebrows rose. "You do?"

"You're thinking that I'm off my rocker, that my cheese has slipped off its cracker, but it's not true."

Jed's lips twitched. "No, ma'am. I understand. Your cheese is still firmly attached to its cracker."

She beamed at him. "That's right." Turning, she reached out to pat Caitlin's arm as she had done with Jed. Her hand was cool. "No. You're wrong. I did the right thing by picking up that penny even though it isn't a penny. It brought me luck. You were there to save me."

Caitlin looked at Jed. This time it was his turn to shrug. "I don't think that was luck," Caitlin said gently.

Reenie's eyes brightened as she turned to Caitlin. "Of course you don't, dear. I'm well aware that you don't really believe in luck, do you? Only in hard work and self-sufficiency."

"Well, I..." Good grief, how had this little lady known that? Caitlin's amazement must have shown on her face, because Jed's grin flickered.

Reenie had her back to him. He lifted his hand and tapped a finger against his temple to indicate what he thought of her mental acuity.

Without turning around, Reenie said, "I thought we'd agreed I'm not crazy, young man. Merely ancient. Be careful, I may think the only gentleman your parents raised was your brother, Steve."

Jed's mouth flopped open and color climbed his cheeks. "I'm sorry, I... How do you know I have a brother named Steve?"

Reenie didn't answer. Instead, she took Caitlin's hand and folded the bottle cap into it. "There, I think you need this. It'll teach you a good lesson." She took the handle of the cart and said, "I must be on my way now. I'll be seeing you again."

Jed recovered his much-vaunted manners and stepped

forward. "Why don't you let us drive you home, Ms. Starr?"

"Now, really," she said in a long-suffering tone. "I'll be very offended if you don't call me by my first name. Otherwise how will I know you're my friend?" She moved away without giving him time to think up an answer. "No thank you, young man. It's not far. Only up Old Barton Road."

Jed frowned. "Only one person lives up Old Barton Road," he said. "And she's gone."

"I know," Reenie answered, and once again started off. "I'm not there yet because I'm still here." Jed and Caitlin exchanged blank stares as Reenie stepped to the curb.

This time, she paused to look both ways before stepping from the curb, but she glanced back to give Caitlin a warm smile. "Your hair looked much better long. I'll bet your young man here thought so, too," she said, nodding at Jed. "It was very soft and feminine. I think he liked to touch it. Men do, you know. My Harvey always said my long curls were my best feature." She touched her hair and regret lined her face for a moment. "But it's easier for me to keep this way, and he's no longer here to care."

Caitlin was startled. Her own short hair was covered by a baseball cap. Questions sprang to her lips, but Reenie was already turning away with a wave. Caitlin watched, dumbfounded, as the tiny figure made her way across the street and down the sidewalk, disappearing around the corner that led to the old gravel road.

"Well, I'll be damned," Jed said, running his hand through his damp hair. "Do you think we just met a witch?"

A shiver ran across Caitlin's shoulders and she glanced uneasily at the bottle cap in her hand, but she said dismissively, "Don't be silly. She's only a sweet old lady. Maybe a little addled."

Jed nodded as he contemplated the direction Reenie had gone. "There really isn't anything down Old Barton Road except my aunt Geneva's house at this end, and we both know she's out of town. There's no one renting her little apartment out back, and my whole family has orders to stay away from there. Says she doesn't want us prowling around. On the cliff at the other end, there's a wrecked farmhouse someone slapped together back in the thirties. Steve and I used to play there as kids. I'm amazed now that the place didn't collapse around our ears. It's got an incredible view. Developers have been coveting it for years. *I've* been coveting it for years, but the owner won't sell, so I know Mrs. Starr can't be living there."

"Well," Caitlin said, still worried, "maybe she's a little confused and will find her way all right." She turned an uncertain gaze on him. "You think so, don't you, Jed?"

His eyes met the worry in hers. "Tell you what," he said briskly. "Let's get in my car and drive up that way, make sure she gets home okay, then we can come back and get your car."

Caitlin sent him a grateful smile. "You're a pal, Jed Bishop."

Jed snorted. "Nicest thing you've said to me in three weeks. If I'd known that was all it took to get you to be reasonable, I would have been trotting little old ladies across every street in Crystal Cove."

"To quote our new friend, 'Don't make me take back what I said'," Caitlin responded, giving him a retiring look. With a quick step, she headed back to his car.

While she was fastening her seat belt, Jed picked up his jumper cables, slammed the hood of her car, then hopped into the seat beside her. They pulled out of MacAllen's parking lot and were soon tooling up the street.

When they turned onto the dirt road, Caitlin sat up straight, looking for Reenie. As they passed Geneva Bishop's closed-up house, they saw that the road ahead of them was empty.

There was no sign of the little old woman even though they drove all the way up to the dead end by the farmhouse with its caved-in roof.

Jed waved his hand toward the open car window. "See, she's not here. She probably got her bearings straight and headed on home."

"I hope you're right." Caitlin looked again at the bottle cap Reenie had given her. She had the unsettling feeling that something important had occurred, but she didn't know why she thought that. That was just a fanciful notion, she told herself as she shoved the bottle cap into her jeans pocket. When she looked up, Jed was studying her.

"Something on your mind?" he asked.

"No, no, not at all," she answered, but his skeptical look told her he didn't believe her. She turned away, wishing she wasn't so easy to read. Or at the very least, she wished things were better balanced and he was as easy to read as she seemed to be.

He should have been, she thought, staring down at her hands resting in her lap. His quick grin and easygoing manner should have been those of a man whose thoughts went no further than tomorrow, or at the most, no further than his Saturday-night date.

It wasn't that way, though, which was why she'd been so off balance since meeting him. Maybe it was also why it had been so easy for him to tumble her into bed—or rather, there had been no tumbling to it. It had been pure finesse.

She might as well face it. She liked things in her life to be well ordered and settled, and he'd been unsettling her from the start.

Jed was still watching her. Caitlin glanced at him, then away from those gray eyes that saw too much. To her relief, he said nothing.

He turned the car around and they went back to the market. He jump-started her car and promised to install a new battery the next day, but Caitlin had to put her foot down when he offered to buy one for her.

"I *always* pay my own way, Jed," she told him bluntly once her car was idling with its usual rumble-and-cough rhythm.

"Yeah, I'm learning that about you." Jed slammed the car hood closed. "I don't know why you won't accept a loan for a car. I know from our partnership papers that you've got a good credit history. The bank would give you a loan in a minute. I've offered several times. I'd do it for any of my friends. I've given dozens of them."

She knew that, and it was another reason she didn't want one. She didn't want to be bailed out like so many other people who depended on him. She realized now that was part of the reason she'd entered into the partnership with him, so that he would see her as a serious businesswoman and not simply another person he needed to rescue. "And I've turned you down several times. I wish I had a new car, but it will have to wait until I can afford it. I won't accept a loan."

"It's only money, Caitlin. It can be paid back."

She didn't know how to answer that. She couldn't argue with his easygoing attitude and she was unwilling to explain her fear of debt. Money wasn't as easy to replace as he seemed to think. Besides, it wasn't the money itself, but the security it offered that appealed to her.

Finally she said, "I'll take care of the battery myself, Jed. Tomorrow."

Surrendering, he held up his hands, but his lips tightened and he shook his head at her stubbornness. "All right, then. Let's go home. I'll be right behind you in case you have any more trouble."

Caitlin nodded her thanks and drove home, aware of him behind her, wishing she wasn't so conflicted about what was right for her—independence—and what she wanted—Jed.

When she reached the old Victorian house, she parked her car, waved her thanks to Jed and hurried inside. She was anxious to take a nice, relaxing bath, put on warm pajamas and fix herself some dinner—not a sandwich tonight, but something hot and nourishing.

However, her phone was ringing when she mounted the stairs and she hurried in to answer it. Her phone rarely rang. Since she was new in Crystal Cove, she knew few people other than her clients, and they never called her at home.

She answered briskly on its fifth ring and a male voice on the other end said, "Ms. Beck? This is Gordon Carrow of Carrow Classic Cars and Auto Restorations."

Caitlin smiled. Maybe he was calling to give her an estimate on restoring her car. Too bad hers wasn't a classic. It was merely a clunker.

Caitlin sat on the sofa with a whoosh of breath. After this afternoon's experience, she sincerely wished she could take this man up on whatever great deal he was no doubt going to offer her. Sighing, she asked, "Yes, Mr. Carrow, what can I do for you?"

"Ms. Beck, it's what I can do for you—or maybe I should say it's what you've done for yourself."

Caitlin rolled her eyes. She really didn't have time for this. She wanted a bath and dinner, but she found it impossible to be rude to people on the phone. She had helped pay her way through college by making unsolicited calls, known as cold calls, for a telemarketing firm. She knew what it was like to have the phone hung up in her ear, so she couldn't do that to this man. She scraped at the bits of mud on her shirt while she waited patiently for the pitch. It wasn't long in coming.

In an excited voice he said, "You, Ms. Caitlin Beck, are the winner in the Crystal Cove Merchants' Harvest Bonanza! Congratulations!"

Caitlin didn't answer, waiting for him to go on.

"Ms. Beck, did you hear me?" he asked hesitantly, some of the excitement draining from his voice.

"Yes, I did, Mr. Carrow. It was very nice of you to call and let me know that. Now, what exactly is it I have to buy in order to win whatever it is I've won?" she asked politely.

There was a lengthy pause. "Uh, miss, I think maybe you're not hearing me. You don't have to buy anything. You signed up for the Harvest Bonanza Grand Giveaway."

Vaguely Caitlin recalled the posters and banners she'd seen around town the past few weeks. They advertised special deals and giveaways at many of the retailers. She couldn't recall signing up for anything, though. Uncertainly she said, "I'll take your word for it, Mr. Carrow."

Although her tentative response probably wasn't what he had expected, Mr. Carrow went on, "Well, anyway, we had the drawing today and you're the proud owner of a fully restored, beautifully reconditioned 1957 Chevrolet Bel-Air."

Caitlin straightened abruptly. "Excuse me?"

"We'd like to bring it over tonight if possible," Mr. Carrow continued. "I've got a video crew all ready to go, so we can tape you receiving the keys. We sponsor the *Midnight Movie* on Channel Six and we'd like to show the tape on our commercials tonight."

Her heart beating fast, Caitlin wheezed, "Is…is this a joke?"

He laughed. "No, I assure you it's no joke. To prove it, we'll be there in an hour with your car." He paused, then added, "If you've got family and friends close by, maybe you'd like to invite them over. They can be in the video, too. Let me confirm your address." He rattled it off and, in a daze, Caitlin confirmed it. With a cheery goodbye, he hung up.

Caitlin sat staring at the receiver. This was incredible. Slowly she replaced the phone and sat trying to recall exactly when she had entered the Bonanza giveaway at Carrow Classic Cars and Auto Restorations. Never. She had never even been there. Of course, she could have signed up at some other merchant in town, but she didn't think so. She never did that sort of thing.

This had to be a hoax. She grabbed the phone book and leafed through it rapidly to find Carrow's phone number. When she called back, the phone was answered by a receptionist who confirmed the information, congratulating Caitlin on her snappy red Bel-Air. "You'll be the envy of your friends," the woman said.

"No kidding," Caitlin breathed. "But I…I don't remember even entering the contest. I only moved here a few months ago."

"Oh, well, that explains it," the woman said breezily.

"Every new resident was entered automatically as a sort of 'welcome to Crystal Cove' gift. There was an announcement in the *Crystal Cove Clarion*."

"I...I guess I didn't see it," Caitlin said faintly. Her mind was spinning. "Well, thank you. Thank you very much."

When she hung up the second time, Caitlin sat stunned for a moment, then jumped straight up off the couch with a crow of joy, threw her hands into the air and did a little jig of delight around the room. She couldn't believe this. She'd never won anything before in her life.

Who could she tell? Her best friends, Tony and Anna Danova, were in San Francisco. She knew hardly anyone here, except for.... Her dance slowed to a stop, her hands fell to her sides, and she looked at her apartment door, imagining the man who was across the hall.

She could tell Jed that she'd won a car, not a new one like he'd been encouraging her to buy, but a classic, a red one, and she had to tell someone or burst with the news.

Before she could give it further thought and talk herself out of being impulsive, she whipped open her door and dashed across the hall. She knocked, then did a fancy little two-step while she waited for him to answer.

When the door opened, she whirled around excitedly to see him standing in the entrance, briskly drying his hair with a small white towel. When he saw her, he looped it around his neck and looked at her with interest.

"Yes, Caitlin?"

She focused on his face. "Jed, you'll never guess..." Her eyes traveled rapidly downward, spied his hands loosely clasping the ends of the towel, framing his chest, sharply defining the muscles there. Then her gaze dropped lower—to his stomach. There were muscles there that she knew from firsthand experience were as hard as a slab of marble.

Completely against her will, her tongue darted out to wet her lips, and her gaze shot back to his face, which was taking on a puzzled look. She hitched in a breath and tried again. "You'll never guess—"

"You said that already," he interrupted in a voice one breath away from a chuckle.

"What...you'll never..." Her words stumbled over themselves, withered up in her desert-dry mouth, then blew away.

While she had been on the phone and then dancing around her apartment, Jed had been in the shower.

He was barefoot, had on jeans, zipped but unbuttoned, and no shirt. The hair that curled across that washboard stomach of his, already dark, was nearly black with dampness. The scent of soap and aftershave eddied out to tantalize her.

An unwanted memory of touching him, being held and loved by him, burst through her. She had tried so hard to suppress that memory, but it had been there all the time, waiting to pop out like a genie from a magic lamp, ready to tempt and torment her. The sight, the scent of him, had desire sifting through her, gathering strength until it kicked her right in the belly, nearly sending her sprawling on her bottom.

Eyes wide, mouth falling softly open, Caitlin looked up at him. Her bottom lip trembled before she bit down on it, bringing it under control.

Jed's politely interested smile underwent a slow, blatant change until it held the usual teasing she knew so well. Being Jed, he knew exactly what her problem was!

"Something wrong, Caitlin?"

She cleared her throat, but still her answer came out as

if someone had stepped on her toe. "No!" She softened her tone. "Uh, I mean, no."

"Do you see something you like?"

Did she ever! Her face turned a bright pink. She was being ridiculous. It certainly wasn't as if she'd never seen him half-dressed—much less than half-dressed—before. She wasn't going to give him the satisfaction of knowing how he was affecting her. She would never hear the end of it.

That thought stiffened her resolve. She had fought this for three weeks now. She knew she could conquer it. Besides, it had been at least an hour since she had passed her limit of thinking about him only ten times a day.

She took a deep breath, but still she stammered when she answered. "I...I just received a call. I...I've won a car."

Jed's face went blank. "You're kidding."

"It's true. Fully restored," she quoted. "Beautifully reconditioned. I'll be the envy of all my friends."

Happiness bubbled through her and she laughed. The expression on Jed's face changed from the teasing look to something more serious, more alert. His eyes sharpened subtly.

Caitlin gave only fleeting notice to it as her explanation tumbled from her. Breathlessly she ran through everything Mr. Carrow had said, concluding with, "...and the receptionist said I was entered automatically as a new resident, and...and I won."

"The Harvest Bonanza Grand Giveaway. I wondered if they had a winner yet."

"They do. Me."

"That's great, Caitlin, " he said, grinning. "Congratulations. I'm certainly envious. Gordie does excellent work."

40   *Meant for You*

"Fully restored," she parroted again, still in something close to shock. She blinked. "Beautifully reconditioned."

Jed laughed, causing her to realize that she was babbling. Blushing, she rolled her eyes comically. He chuckled again, then his brow creased.

"It must be the luck that old lady was talking about," he speculated in a thoughtful tone as he crossed his arms over his chest and leaned against the doorjamb.

"Old lady?" Caitlin's eyes glazed at the sight of those spectacular muscles that bunched and stretched when he crossed his arms. She almost wished he wouldn't stand like that, but if he didn't how could she enjoy this show?

"The old lady at MacAllen's," Jed responded. "She said it would teach you a good lesson."

"MacAllen's?" she asked, finally lifting dazed eyes away from his magnificent pecs to focus on his face. He was watching her with that knowing smile of his.

"Oh!" Caitlin slapped her hand against her jeans pocket. The bottle cap was still there. She drew it out and flipped it in the air. It's shiny surface caught the reflection from the hall light, winking tantalizingly at her. She caught it and examined it for a moment. It was only a flattened bottle cap, after all. Some of her excitement began to cool. "I don't think so, Bishop," she said briskly. "It's a coincidence."

"Oh, that's right. You're the one who doesn't believe in luck."

That was before she had won a car, she thought. "I only said I believe more in hard work than in luck."

Jed's grin kicked up one corner of his mouth. "But this time, it's luck, not hard work that brought you what you needed. Maybe Reenie Starr *is* a witch," he concluded. "After all, you did wish for a new car."

"Oh, come on, Jed. It's not like a fairy godmother suddenly appeared to grant my wish. Saying I wished I had a car was...the kind of thing...anyone would say under the circumstances." She flapped her hand at him. "Oh, never mind. Bishop, I'm not going to get into this discussion. I've got to go get ready. They're bringing the car tonight and they're going to videotape it for a television advertisement."

"But first, you came to tell me. Caitlin, I'm touched."

"Don't be," she said repressively. She realized with relief that she was getting her equilibrium back. A little teasing from Jed put her right back where she should be—businesslike, responsible, totally unaffected by the sight of his tousled hair, sexy grin and bare chest. Totally unaffected, she assured herself, taking another quick inventory. And that odd warmth she was feeling was hunger. After all, she'd had no dinner. The fact that the warmth wasn't in her stomach, but in a place a little bit lower that was strictly feminine didn't mean a thing. Congratulating herself on that bit of logic, she lifted her gaze to meet his again. "Mr. Carrow told me he would be here in an hour and I should invite my friends to be in the video and..."

Darn! Why had she let herself in for this? Thinking of Jed as a friend was only going to get her into something she certainly didn't want.

Jed straightened, his gray eyes gleaming. "When Gordie and the video crew are gone, we should celebrate."

"No," she snapped, remembering how their last celebration had gotten so out of hand. "After they're gone, I'm taking my new car for a drive, and—"

"You want me to be your first passenger." Laughing softly, Jed stepped toward her. "That's the best offer I've had all day."

"It wasn't an offer, I... Oh, forget it!" Whirling around, she rushed to her apartment, had a short tussle with the balky knob, then whirled inside and slammed the door.

3

JED SHRUGGED and stepped back into his own apartment, shoving the door shut with his elbow.

Hell's bells, he never knew where he was with her. He shook his head as he headed into his bedroom to finish dressing. That wasn't true, he thought. With her, he was out of her life, across the hall, out in the cold, *way* out in the cold.

He reached for his shirt, put it on, and began buttoning it with quick little twists of his wrist. He had no one to blame but himself. Two months ago he had taken one look at her and pure lust had raised its insidious head. Damn. He could have sworn he'd conquered that devil when he was about twenty-two.

Then, when she'd opened her mouth and started talking and he'd realized there was an actual brain inside that beautiful head, he'd completely lost it.

Jed tucked in his shirt, then smoothed his hair. He was the first to admit that he liked women. Okay. To tell the truth, he loved women, and he'd never had much trouble attracting them because they seemed to like him, too.

Caitlin had been a challenge, though. Right from the beginning, when he'd seen her in her office dressed in one of her San Francisco financial-district power suits, he'd been intrigued. His younger sister, Diana, said there was an indefinable quality that showed whether or not a woman had class. He'd never known what that meant until he'd met Caitlin, with her sleek chestnut hair curving around her chin, her big golden-brown eyes staring at him through the lenses of those reading glasses she affected, in hopes, he was sure, of making herself look less feminine and desirable. It hadn't worked. He would have found her desirable if she'd been dressed in a gunnysack.

He had only gone into her office that day to introduce himself and talk to her a bit. His imperious aunt Geneva had called from Los Angeles, where she was visiting friends, to say she had a little nest egg to invest and had heard there was a new investment counselor in Crystal Cove. A woman. Geneva had assigned him the task of finding out if Caitlin seemed trustworthy.

He could have given Aunt Geneva the advice she needed, but despite the fact that she had three brothers and numerous nephews, she didn't much like men. She had never married or had any inclination to do so, and whenever possible had sought out women in any profession she dealt with. Until recently she had taken the advice of a male stockbroker. However, now that there was a woman available, she insisted that she wanted a woman's advice. As ordered, he'd gone to obtain one of the brochures that detailed Caitlin's experience in financial matters and her philosophy about investing.

As it turned out, he'd picked up the brochure to send to his aunt and he'd convinced Caitlin to have lunch with him. They had talked about common stocks, mutual funds and investment portfolios while his ungovernable imagination had been picturing her talking about other things, her full lips welcoming him to her, her eyes dark with promise, with passion. In his mind, he saw her reaching for him.

Quite a leap, considering that sitting at one of the small

tables at Margie's Café, all he'd been able to see of her were her hands, face and satiny throat.

It was the voice that had come out of that throat that had captured him, along with her serious expression, accented by occasional flashes of humor and a vulnerability in her eyes that she masked with a businesslike manner.

On the spot he'd come up with his crazy plan to get her to invest in the house he was renovating—though he certainly hadn't needed an investor. He'd guessed right away that she wouldn't let him get close to her for the normal man/woman reasons, so he'd scrambled around for another one. Using the house had seemed logical. It was an excellent investment.

Jed grimaced. It was true that his plans occasionally didn't work out as he'd thought they would. Diana said it was because he didn't consider the consequences, but she was wrong. It was only that the consequences sometimes caught up with him before he was ready for them.

A prime example was the partnership with Caitlin.

He saw now that she really hadn't the money to spare, but once she'd seen the old house, she had fallen in love with it. Even then, she'd tried to be practical, reasoning that she shouldn't invest on a whim, that such a move would make her look untrustworthy to her clients. He'd finally convinced her, though, that the money would be an investment in her future. He'd had to promise that she could get out of the deal whenever she wanted. She didn't want out of the deal now, though. She wanted to buy *him* out, making payments that would fit into her budget. She'd even been determined to forgo a new car to do it.

He had thought he was making real progress, especially when they'd consummated their partnership, so to speak, but she had awakened the next morning with a panicked look in her eyes. That was when good old Mr. Consequences had kicked him in the butt. With breathless excuses and apologies, she had dashed from his apartment into hers while he'd hopped along behind her demanding explanations while trying to get into his skivvies.

Since that morning, she had kept him at a distance. In his opinion she had reacted in a way that was completely out of proportion to what had gone on between them.

Not that it hadn't been good, Jed thought as he reached for his keys and pocket change. In fact, it had been damned good. He wouldn't mind repeating the experience every night for a while. After that, they would be good friends. That was how it had worked out with all the previous women in his life. He liked it that way. However, this particular woman wasn't so inclined.

That was when he'd finally understood that Caitlin Beck might be a successful career woman with brains and ambition, but she had secrets he hadn't expected. As far as he was concerned, that wasn't fair. He'd always been involved with uncomplicated women before. Mostly they had been interested in one of two things: a good time or a good husband. He was still friends with most of the women in the first group and he'd managed to deflect those in the second group to a male acquaintance interested in the husband part.

It hadn't taken him long to realize that he'd made a bad mistake by rushing Caitlin; he should have wooed and coaxed her. He knew women needed time, finesse, romance. He knew that, but he'd rushed her, anyway.

When she had begun insisting she would buy out his half of their renovation project, he had actually been given a little hope. After all, she wouldn't be so insistent if she was apathetic toward him.

Still, he had been confused, so he had switched modes and begun treating her with the same teasing attitude he used with his sisters and his old girlfriends, but hell, that wasn't working, either. She had a breezy answer for every one of his teasing remarks. When she got home, she ducked into her apartment across the hall and he didn't see her unless he bullied his way in—which he had begun doing every night.

Maybe it was only his ego doing his thinking for him, but he couldn't help the feeling that the way she had pulled back and begun avoiding him didn't really involve him entirely. There was something else going on that he couldn't quite get a handle on. Lately he'd been thinking that there must be a man back in San Francisco she was still involved with.

Ego talking again, he thought ruefully—she had to be involved with someone else or she wouldn't be so reluctant to become involved with him. He was old enough to know that if a woman wasn't interested, she simply wasn't interested, but he didn't think that was it. After all, he'd seen the look in her eyes when he'd opened the door. She wasn't as immune to him as she pretended.

Still, he ought to be ashamed of the way he kept pushing himself into her life. His only excuse was that she was a puzzle that intrigued him.

He'd always been a sucker for puzzles.

Jed rolled his shoulders, trying to ease the tension there as he told himself to forget her for a little while. He was expected at his folks' house, along with the rest of the family, for their regular monthly dinner. If he didn't show up, his mother would arrive on his doorstep with concern and a quart of chicken soup.

A smile glimmered in his eyes as he thought about asking Caitlin to go with him, but she had resisted all his attempts to get her to meet his family. Besides, she was going to be busy in about forty-five minutes taking delivery on one of Gordie's cars, one of those for which good old Gordie usually received as much as fifty thousand dollars. He would love to know how the Chamber of Commerce had talked Gordie into donating it.

If she was a normal red-blooded American girl—and despite recent indications to the contrary, he knew she was—Caitlin was going to love that car.

Jed paused as he was reaching for his car keys. He recalled the look of uncomplicated delight in Caitlin's eyes. She'd won a car and he'd been the first one she'd told.

Running his hand over his chin, Jed considered how he could use this situation to his advantage. She had no family here, or anywhere, as far as he could determine. Since she was new in town, she had few friends yet. It would look good if there was a cheering crowd around when she took possession of her new set of wheels.

With a calculating grin, Jed reached for the phone.

WHAT DID ONE WEAR to accept delivery of a gift of a classic car worth thousands of dollars? Caitlin wondered as she stood surveying the contents of her closet. Slacks were out. Her last clean pair was now spotted with muddy water. A suit wouldn't work. Those were only for work, and Jed had told her they made her look unapproachable and as humorless as a tax collector with an ax to grind.

She would show him. Caitlin reached far back into her closet and pulled out a dress of electric blue she'd bought when Anna Danova had bet her that she didn't have the nerve to wear it. Her friend had been right. It had hung in her closet for nearly a year.

Holding it up and viewing it with a critical eye, Caitlin realized that the dress wasn't anything fancy, but its fitted waist and slim skirt weren't her usual style. Neither was the V-neck that cried out for a glittering necklace. In fact, it was very nearly a party dress, and she almost always stuck to business attire.

She reached up, intending to put it back, but then muttered, "Oh, why not?" It wasn't every day that she won a new car, or anything else for that matter. She wasn't a risk taker. Caitlin thought about her night with Jed. Well, maybe she was an occasional risk taker.

Exasperated with her waffling, she pulled the dress on, figuring it would probably be a very long time before she had a better opportunity to wear it.

A few minutes later she was standing before the mirror checking her hair and makeup when she heard cars coming up the circular drive. She flew to the window, straining to see her new car through the gathering dusk. But her apartment was at the corner of the house and the window afforded only a glimpse of the driveway, so she couldn't see much except for a line of cars. How many people was Mr. Carrow bringing with him, anyway?

Too excited to wait for them to ring the doorbell and fearful they might trip over the piles of building materials in the entryway, Caitlin rushed from her apartment. She flew down the stairs so fast they barely had time to creak. She heard Jed's door open as she hurried, and knew that he was following. He was always around, giving her his advice and opinions, so why should she think tonight would be any different? This time, though, she was glad he would be there. She wanted to share this moment with someone.

When she reached the bottom of the stairs, she scrambled across the entryway, then stood for a second with her hand pressed to her stomach while she regained her breath. Finally she walked sedately to the door and opened it, aiming a warm but professional smile at the person who stood there.

Caitlin's smile sagged and she had to drop her gaze ten inches to make eye contact with her visitor. This wasn't Mr. Carrow. It was a girl of about eleven who had a mouthful of braces and an armload of accordion. As soon as she spied Caitlin, she grinned hugely, hitched up her instrument and swung into a loud, off-key rendition of "Roll out the Barrel."

The noise was teeth-gratingly awful.

Stunned, Caitlin stared down at the little girl who was running her fingers over the keyboard, only hitting about every third note correctly and compressing the squeeze box with cheerful enthusiasm. She was working so hard at her music that the tip of her tongue could be seen caught between her silver-lined front teeth.

Whoever this girl was, she looked so endearing that Caitlin didn't have the heart to follow her first inclination and clap her hands over her ears. The child broke her concentration for a second and looked up at Caitlin with another grin.

Caitlin's eyes narrowed. Where had she seen that grin before?

Its twin appeared over her right shoulder as Jed came up behind her and put his arm around her waist. "Hi, Jessie," he said to the little girl. "Sounds great. Those lessons are really paying off." He looked past her. "Where are your mom and dad?"

The girl broke off her playing in midsquawk. "Hi, Uncle Jed. Dad said I should bring this to provide the music for the party. He said everyone should get the pleasure of listening, not just him and mom."

Jed cleared his throat and Caitlin knew he was swallowing a laugh. "Your dad is all heart."

"He told me you'd say that." She nodded back over her shoulder. "Here they come. Mom needs help getting out of the car now." She gave Caitlin a frankly curious look. "Is this the lady who won the car?"

"Yes." Stepping from behind Caitlin, Jed urged her forward. "Caitlin Beck, this is my niece, Jessica Bishop. You'll meet the rest of my family in about two minutes."

Caitlin, always scrupulously polite, except perhaps with Jed, could only nod at the girl before her gaze dropped once again to her instrument. Taking that as her cue, Jessica whipped into another spirited number—"When the Saints Go Marching In." It didn't sound much better than the last song. Grinning, Jessie marched into the house.

This time Caitlin couldn't help wincing.

Jed looked down at her. "She's barely started lessons," he said by way of explanation.

"I thought so," she answered in a mild tone. "Uh, Jed? Why the accordion? It doesn't seem like something that would interest most girls her age."

"Jessie's not like most girls. She thinks it'll help build up her chest."

"*What?*"

"Seriously. She's afraid of being flat-chested, so she took up the accordion."

"You're making that up."

"It's the truth. She considered the tuba for a while, but I told her about a girl I used to date who played the trombone. It didn't work out, though. All that lung power she had built up made her hard to kiss. The suction was incredible."

"Jed! You didn't say that to your niece."

His eyes twinkled. "Hey, what kind of uncle would I be if I let her play an instrument that might ruin her future love life?"

Caitlin tried to sputter out an answer, but he distracted her by pointing to the front yard. "Here comes the rest of the crew."

Caitlin's eyes lifted and darted around the yard where cars were being parked every which way. People began pouring out of the vehicles and streaming toward her. Everyone seemed to be carrying plastic containers, trays or paper bags.

She finally found her voice. "Jed, why is your family...?" Finally her brain caught up with her ears and she recalled what Jessica had said. "Party?" she asked, turning to him. "Jessica mentioned a party. *What* party?"

"For you," he said. "It's not every day a friend of mine wins something like this, Cait, so I called all of them to come take a look. I knew you wouldn't mind."

"You take a great deal for granted, Bishop."

Unrepentant, he nodded. "It's one of my more endearing qualities. Besides," he added, "you're dressed for it. I've never seen you wear anything like this before." He reached up and ran the tip of his finger beneath the hem of her sleeve. "Nice."

Before his touch could build up any serious shivers in her, Jed moved past her to help a very pregnant woman who had paused at the bottom of the stairs. She seemed to be gathering her strength to make the climb. Jed hurried down and put his hand under her elbow. "Hi, Mary. How's it going?"

"I wish it would go," she sighed, leaning on his arm and resting a hand on her tummy. "If this pregnancy lasts much longer, these babies will be born big enough to play soccer."

He put his arm around her and gave her a sympathetic squeeze, then looked up at Caitlin. "This is my sister-in-law, Mary, and my brother, Steve."

Mary gasped out a hello and congratulations as she gave Caitlin a warm handshake and went inside in search of a place to sit down. Steve, who looked like a slightly older, but more serious version of Jed, followed with a couple of bottles of wine tucked under his arm and a cake balanced on one hand.

"Head on into the parlor," Jed called after them. "There's a chair for Mary and boxes for everyone else to sit on. We can set up sawhorses and planks for tables."

"The parlor?" Caitlin asked, aghast. "That place is a mess."

"Well, where do you suggest? Your apartment is too small and you've avoided coming into mine like you think I'm going to grab you and ravish you right there on the floor. Besides, Mary couldn't make it up those stairs. The doctor says it's twins."

More questions popped into Caitlin's mind, but she didn't have time to ask them because she was busy meeting Jed's mother, Laura, and his father, Dave, his sister, Hailey, her fiancé, Aaron, and his two uncles, Frank and Burton.

"I've got another sister, Diana, but she lives in Sacramento."

Caitlin, who was having her hand squeezed and her arm pumped by his uncle Burton, answered with a dazed nod. "Oh, well, that's too bad."

He laughed.

Everyone was carrying some type of food or drink. Jed's mother even had a tablecloth, a stack of paper plates and napkins, and bags of plastic dinnerware.

Caitlin couldn't remember the last time someone had done something so nice for her, and she didn't know what to say, but it looked as though she wouldn't need to say anything. Jed was pointing toward the driveway.

"Here comes Gordie with your car and his video crew. Hop on out there and I'll get my family to be your cheering section."

Moving at a trot, Jed ducked into the house while Caitlin whirled around to catch sight of her new vehicle. Her eyes strained in the fading light, but her breath stuck in her throat when she saw the beautiful two-tone car, white on top and candy-apple-red on the lower half. Majestically it made the sweeping turn to the front of the house. She was grateful to note that the driver was careful to avoid the potholes in the asphalt. She would hate to see the Bel-Air lose one of its wire wheel covers.

Eagerly she descended the steps as the car reached the front of the house, followed by a minivan that had a man with a video camera hanging out the window. He swung the camera around and pointed it directly at her, filming as she watched the classic Chevrolet come to a stop.

Caitlin fell hopelessly in love with this marvel of Detroit car-making ingenuity. Besides its perfect, shiny paint job and glistening wire wheel covers, she could see that the inside was elegantly upholstered in purest white.

Excitement bubbled through her as she rushed toward Gordon Carrow, who was stepping out, smiling at her. He was a short, wiry man in his fifties who wore a dark suit, a white shirt and a natty bow tie. He was holding the keys in his hand. As soon as she approached, he tossed them into the air jauntily and caught them with a snap.

"You must be Caitlin Beck," he said. "The Crystal Cove merchants are happy to present you with the prize in this year's Bonanza Giveaway." With a flourish of his wrist, he indicated the car.

"I'm happy to receive it," she gulped, and he smiled. As the video crew poured out of their van, he turned and gave them some instructions. At the same time, Jed's family came out of the house, congratulating her and exclaiming over her good fortune. The cameraman nearly tripped over himself as he filmed the Bishops' reactions.

Waving his arms and shouting instructions at the Bishops, Gordon Carrow organized them so that, the tape rolling all the while, they were clapping enthusiastically as he turned the keys over to Caitlin. She accepted with stammered thanks, and the Bishop family surged forward to get a better view of the car.

After asking permission of the dazed new owner, Jed's father, brother and uncles opened the hood to inspect the engine. The women gave it a cursory look, then leaned in the windows to examine the inside.

In the melee, Caitlin found herself pushed up against Jed, who put his arm around her protectively.

Gordon Carrow shouted, "We need something for a grand finale."

Jed growled, "It's a thirty-second commercial, Gordie, not a production of *Grease*."

Gordon wasn't listening. He wrinkled his brow and scratched his head, obviously deep in serious thought. "Something dramatic," he muttered. "Something that will make viewers of the *Midnight Movie* sit up and take notice—remember Carrow Classic Cars and Auto Restorers."

"Gordie, those viewers are mostly insomniacs. They're a captive audience. They won't care."

Gordon gave him an injured look.

"Oh, for Pete's sake," Jed said. He put his hands on Caitlin's shoulders and whirled her around. "How about this, Gordie?"

He bent Caitlin back over his arm theatrically and pressed his lips to hers.

"Perfect," Gordon squealed excitedly. "Roll the tape. Roll the tape!"

The tape rolled, Gordon Carrow shouted enthusiastically, the video crew whistled in appreciation, the entire Bishop family turned to watch, and Caitlin's world spun out of control.

All she could do was clutch at Jed's shoulders and hang on for the ride. And a wild one it was. It could have been a chaste kiss played up only for the camera. With Jed in charge, it became a slick, sensual meeting of breath, then mouths, then, when his tongue traced the seam made by her closed lips and they shuddered open, of tongues as well.

She should stop this, Caitlin thought hazily, even as she felt Jed's hands skim over her back, pulling her in closer. Her own hands shot up to circle his back where she could feel the muscles bunch and strain against her palms.

Oh, she didn't want this, she thought as she met him touch for touch. She didn't want to remember what it had been like, to remember how badly she had needed him and how wonderful it had felt to be taken by him.

Finally he raised his head, and even though it was almost full dark now, the light from the video camera still shone on him and she could see the glittering triumph reflected in his eyes.

Caitlin pushed at his shoulders and he swept her back to her feet as the light from the camera cut off.

Head spinning, she turned blindly to Gordon. "Please don't...don't use that," she said breathlessly, stumbling away from Jed.

"Nonsense," the spry little man said. "It'll make a great ending."

Caitlin gave him a furious look, then turned her ire on

Jed. "I have a professional image to maintain, Jed. What will my clients think when they see that?"

Jed shrugged. "Lucky, lucky girl?" he asked innocently.

"Oh, you're impossible."

"So I've been told. Listen, why don't we worry about this later? I'll bet Gordie's got some papers for you to sign, and you probably want to take your new car for a ride."

Since she was already the center of interest for the entire crowd, Caitlin decided to let the matter drop until they were alone. Besides, she *was* eager to take her new car for a drive.

Pointedly she turned away from him to finish her business with the car dealer. As soon as that was done, Gordon and the camera crew packed up and prepared to leave. Caitlin dashed upstairs for a jacket, then invited the Bishop women to accompany her on her maiden voyage.

As they drove away, Jed's mother leaned out the window and insisted that the men get the food ready while they were gone.

It took Caitlin a few minutes to get the feel of the car. It was so much bigger and more powerful than her little compact. After driving a few miles, she turned the car around carefully and drove back to the house. She dropped off the women and picked up the men, except for Jed who said he would wait. The Bishop men all looked as if they would love nothing more than to be behind the wheel of the car themselves, but they didn't ask, which Caitlin took as a sign that their manners were better than Jed's.

By the time she returned from the second trip, Caitlin felt more confident about handling the car, but she was still cautious.

She parked in front of the house and they all streamed inside to eat. Caitlin was impressed by the flexibility of the family. They didn't seem to mind serving themselves from a makeshift table consisting of boards perched on two sawhorses, sitting on top of boxes of floor tiles and eating from plates balanced on their laps.

They were genuinely nice people who were as pleased with her good fortune as she was. Caitlin found herself envying Jed his family.

It was quite late before everyone left, and Caitlin closed the door behind them with a happy smile. She turned from the entryway to find Jed right behind her.

"Got the keys to your new car?" he asked.

"Of course." She pulled them from the pocket of the jacket she'd left by the front door.

"Then it's my turn for a ride."

"Forget it, Bishop," she said automatically, slipping them back into the pocket and folding the jacket over her arm.

He walked toward her, hands outstretched innocently. "Hey, I'm not asking to drive."

"Yet," she added sardonically.

He stopped before her, tucked his hands into the back pockets of his jeans and bounced on his toes. "I'm not going to point out that you owe me."

"What for?"

"Inviting my family over so you'd have some friends around."

"Well, then, thanks Jed." There was no denying that she had genuinely enjoyed meeting them. "But I didn't realize you had invited them so you could blackmail me into getting a ride in my car."

His forehead creased in irritation. "Why do you insist

on putting the worst possible spin on everything I say and do?"

Shamed, she knew it was a defense mechanism. Maybe an unfair one. Glancing away, she cleared her throat. "Sorry."

"You're forgiven. Let's go."

She could have put her foot down and told him no, but she knew that would be petty. She did manage to give him a pointed look and say, "All right, but I'm driving."

"Whatever you say, ma'am," Jed answered, hustling her out the door.

Caitlin tried to give Jed the same kind of cautious ride she had given his family members, but once they pulled onto the highway, he said, "Honey, quit driving like a little old lady."

"I'm not going to drive like you do!"

"You've got a V-8 engine in this thing powerful enough to blast you to the moon. Why don't you open her up and see what she can do?"

Caitlin gripped the wheel and gave him a sideways glance.

"Chicken?" he taunted.

"Of course not," she answered. "I simply don't see the need. That would be dangerous."

"There's no one on this road," he said, cutting her off and spreading his hands wide to indicate the empty highway that stretched before them. It was one of the few straight sections on the coast. "Do it for fun. Quit analyzing things for once and do it."

Stung, she turned with a flounce and faced the road. She punched down on the accelerator, the classic car bucked, then took off with a deep-throated roar.

"That's more like it," Jed crowed in triumph. He settled back, propped his right arm in the window, stretched his left one along the back of the bench seat and relaxed.

Caitlin spared him a glance again and decided that with his black hair flying in the wind blasting in the open window and his triumphant grin stretched from ear to ear, he looked for all the world like the king of the road.

As they sped along, her initial caution gave way to a pure sense of thrill at the car's power. It was fun, for once, to put aside her usual prudence and be a bit reckless.

She laughed out loud, causing Jed to lean over and grip her shoulder in shared excitement.

"Come on, I bet she can do even better than this."

Recklessly encouraged, she pressed her foot down on the accelerator a bit more.

Heady with excitement, she laughed and glanced in the rearview mirror.

That was when she saw the flashing blue and yellow lights.

4

CAITLIN'S JOY DIED an instant death and her heart jumped into her throat, where it stuck like a giant gumball. Immediately her foot slammed onto the brake, and the car began coasting to a stop. It took longer for her to slow the massive vehicle than it ever had with her Nissan. She had a moment's panicked thought that the officer might think she was deliberately stalling. As she steered the car onto the shoulder of the road, she cast a fiery look at Jed.

"'An engine in this thing that could blast me to the moon? Open her up and see what she can do'?" she quoted furiously as she shut off the engine and fumbled for the emergency brake. "Well, now we know, don't we? She can get a ticket."

Jed looked behind them. "Hey, it doesn't have to be a ticket. You can probably get by with only a warning if you know how to talk your way out of this."

"Talk my way out of it?" she asked incredulously.

"Sure. You have to know how to do it right."

"And I'll bet you're going to tell me, too, aren't you? Save your breath. I don't need any more advice from you." She began searching through the jacket pocket where she'd put her wallet.

"Hey, it's probably Don Brentanski. He loves pretty women. All you have to do is smile at him the right way and he's putty in your hands."

Caitlin's eyes narrowed. "Are you suggesting I use *sex* to keep from getting a ticket?"

"Hell, no. I'm not saying you need to sleep with the guy. Just be nice to him."

"That's disgusting!" She stuck her nose in the air. "I will treat him with professional courtesy and I'm sure he'll treat me the same way."

Jed flicked his hands as if washing them of this situation. "All the same, it wouldn't hurt to take my advice. First of all, get out of the car slowly and carefully and walk back to meet him with your license and registration in your hand. Admit you made a mistake. Smile, apologize, tell him it's all my fault if you want to, and he'll go easy on you."

"The only mistake I made was listening to you in the first place!" she shot back as the patrol car came to a stop behind her. She glanced in her rearview mirror and saw that the officer was writing something. Her license-plate number, no doubt. She turned back to Jed as she jerked her thumb to indicate the patrolman. "I'm not going to jump out and go sashaying back there like I'm trying to flirt my way out of this."

Jed looked as if she'd injured him. "A little flirting never hurt."

"I'm going to forget you said that." She tossed her hair, then recalled it was now too short to toss. She ignored Jed as she planned how she was going to deal with this. She drummed her fingers on the steering wheel. "I've never been stopped for speeding before or for any other traffic violation. If I tell the patrolman that, I'm sure he'll understand."

"He might, but I know Brentanski. He'd like it a lot better if that information was delivered with a warm... smile."

Caitlin fumed as she waited for the officer to get out of his car and approach her. Why had she listened to Jed? Why did her common sense always seem to take a vacation when she was around him?

"Come on, what can it hurt?" Jed urged. "I admit I got you into this, so I'm simply trying to give you some advice to talk yourself out of it. Get out of the car, smile, be friendly, turn on the charm. Assuming you've got any," he added dryly.

Caitlin's eyes snapped at him, but she found herself actually considering it. After all, she'd never been in this situation before. He might know what he was talking about. If she didn't try this and ended up with a ticket for speeding, he would say she should have tried his method. Either way, she couldn't win.

Grabbing her wallet out of her jacket pocket, she reached for the door handle. "All right," she said. "But this better work."

"I guarantee it."

"Ha!"

Forgetting what Jed had said about moving slowly and carefully, Caitlin whirled out of the car, erupting onto the shoulder of the road as if she'd been catapulted from a slingshot. Her foot landed in a pothole, snapping the heel off her pump. She staggered a few steps, jerked her foot out of the shoe and looked down, astounded, at her stockinged toes. When she bent to pick up the shoe, she overbalanced and had to do a hopping dance to keep from falling face first.

"O-o-o-o-h!" she raged, grabbing the shoe and jamming it back on her foot. Disgusted, she kicked the broken heel aside.

"Miss, have you been drinking?" the officer asked as he approached.

Startled, Caitlin looked up to meet his stern gaze. She snapped to attention and tried to manufacture the serious demeanor of a Supreme Court justice. "No! Certainly not."

"How much alcohol have you consumed tonight?" he asked as he lifted his powerful flashlight and shone it in her face.

"None." Stunned, Caitlin blinked at him. Realizing he was serious, she beat down a spark of panic and said, "I swear, Officer. I haven't been drinking anything stronger than iced tea."

He swept his light over her blue dress. "Looks like you've been to a party."

Caitlin straightened her spine, wishing the low neckline could magically roll up to cover her throat. Hastily she began buttoning her jacket over her chest. Then, afraid she'd made herself appear guilty, she put her chin up in hopes of appearing assertive. "Well, I have, in a way, but—"

"But there was no drinking?" he scoffed.

"Well, there was, but I didn't drink."

He gave her a suspicious look. "I guess we'll find out when I give you the Breathalyzer test. Could I see your driver's license and car registration, please?"

"Of course. I'm perfectly willing to cooperate." Caitlin fumbled in her jacket. She dropped her wallet, swiped it up from the ground, only to drop it again. Muttering under her breath, she took a firm grip on it, removed her license and handed it over.

He took it, studied it, examined her face, studied the photo again. She repressed a hysterical laugh. She could see that his name was indeed Brentanski, and he had all the necessities for dealing with the criminal element—gun, mace, nightstick. He looked like a giant, a long, lean, tough arm of the law—and totally devoid of a sense of humor, not that she was tempted to start cracking jokes. And she certainly wasn't going to try Jed's suggestion and begin flirting!

Caitlin stood at attention and tried her best to look like a responsible citizen. Behind her, she heard the other car door open. She glanced up to see Jed. He gave her a sharp nod and a frown as he mouthed, "Smile," at her.

At least that was what she thought he said since she couldn't see him well in the strobelike brightness from the patrol car's bubble lights. She wrinkled her nose and stuck her tongue out at him exactly when Brentanski lifted his head. The officer gave her a startled look. She closed her mouth and looked up as if studying the stars.

"Hello, Brent," Jed said, clearing his throat. Caitlin knew he was trying to swallow a laugh. "Nice night, isn't it?"

Caitlin instantly decided that if he was laughing at her, she was going to strangle him when they got back in the car—if she wasn't on her way to jail by then.

The officer looked up. "That depends, Jed. It's not a good night for drinking and driving, if that's what you've been doing."

Jed leaned on the car and rested his forearms on the roof. He gave the other man an easy grin. "No, no, Brent. We'd never do that. Why, Miss Beck here hardly ever drinks alcohol. She's very careful about what she drinks."

Caitlin frowned at Jed and said through her teeth, "I'm sure Officer Brentanski isn't interested in that, Jed." If she didn't shut him up, he would probably blurt out that half a bottle of champagne, however, was enough to talk her into bed.

"Sure he is, Cait. The more responsible citizens we have in Crystal Cove, the easier his job will be." He turned back to the officer. "Miss Beck is new to Crystal Cove. She's opened her own business as an investment counselor. In fact, she helped your aunt, Emma Harbel, today. She's going to put her money in some mutual funds and annuities."

Caitlin stared. How had Jed known that? He circled the nose of the car to stand beside her. Again he mouthed, "smile," at her, then lifted his shoulder and winked at her, giving her the cue to flirt with Brent. She raised her hand and formed a fist, but he grasped it in his and held it between them.

"Oh, yeah?" Brent asked, pausing in his examination of Caitlin's license. "What kind of mutual funds and annuities?"

"Low risk, I assure you," Caitlin said hastily as she tried to work her fist out of Jed's grasp. Failing that, she elbowed him in the ribs. He bent over with a whoosh of breath. Satisfied that she'd hurt him, she managed to smile weakly as she spoke to the patrolman. "Your aunt's money will be completely safe."

Brentanski's palm rested on the handle of his gun. He had thick, dark eyebrows that formed a straight line over his eyes. When they drew together, Caitlin was reminded of an approaching thunderstorm. "That money better not be from Uncle Tip's life-insurance policy. She was supposed to let my wife have that to start up a mushroom-growing business. We were going to build sheds out back of our house."

Caitlin's smile collapsed. The money *had* been from Tip Harbel's insurance, but Caitlin wouldn't tell Brent that because of client confidentiality. All she could say was, "Oh?" but her crestfallen expression gave her away.

"Well, hell," the officer groused. "Thanks a lot. Now I'm going to have to go to the bank and get the money."

He fixed Caitlin with a malevolent glare. "Can I see your registration, please?"

Before she could answer, the other door of the patrol car opened and a man climbed out. "Okay if I join you, Brent?" he asked, sauntering forward.

Heck yes, Caitlin thought. *Let's make it a foursome. The more the merrier.* Maybe her good friend Jed would say something to make this newcomer think she was an ax murderer.

When Brentanski stepped back to speak to the man, she looked over at Jed. "Will you please shut up?" she hissed. "And let go of my hand."

"I was only trying to help," he answered in an insulted tone. "And I'm holding your hand so you won't deck me. Policemen don't like rude motorists."

"So far, you've *helped* him think I'm a drunk and a thief trying to do his wife out of her business, and I'm not being rude to *him*, you're—"

"Hello, Al," Jed said. His gaze flashed to Caitlin's angry face. "Caitlin Beck, this is Al Gresham, editor and publisher of the *Crystal Cove Clarion.*"

"Also chief reporter and photographer," the man said cheerfully.

Caitlin looked down and to her horror saw that the man carried a camera. She prayed he wouldn't decide to take her photograph and plaster it all over the weekly paper beneath a headline reading, Financial Adviser Picks up Hints on Local Traffic Laws.

"How do you do?" she asked in a sinking voice. Could this night get any worse? She'd gone from the peak of happiness to the gutter of indignity in only seconds, thanks to her own foolishness in listening to Jed. She gave her hand a sudden twist and managed to get it away from him.

"Your registration, Ms. Beck?" the officer prompted.

Holding her head high, she turned away and limped to the car, where she opened the glove compartment. It was empty, as clean as the windswept prairie. Her luck—if she believed in luck—seemed to be continuing its downward spiral. There was no registration form. Hadn't there been one in all those papers she'd signed for Gordon Carrow? She couldn't remember.

Swearing under her breath, she stood, manufactured a cheery smile and said brightly, "I could run it by your office in the morning, Officer Brentanski, because it doesn't appear to be here."

He seemed to swell indignantly, rocking up on his toes and tucking his tongue into his cheek as he considered her. "Where would it appear to be?" he asked. "You're aware, aren't you, that you're supposed to carry your registration in your vehicle at all times?"

"And I do. Oh, I do," she assured him as embarrassment broke over her in a tidal wave. "At least, I always carry it in my car, my old car. I mean, my other car," she babbled. "But you see, I only got this car a little while ago, and—"

"She got it off Gordie's lot," Jed supplied.

"Gordie's?" Brentanski's eyes narrowed as they swept over the classic car. "You two didn't take one of Gordie's cars, did you, for a little joyriding? Maybe a little necking in the woods?"

"Necking?" Jed hooted. "Brent, are you stuck in the sixties? We're not a couple of teenagers."

"You know what I mean," the officer said.

Caitlin rolled her eyes. "No, Officer Brentanski, we aren't doing anything illegal."

"Except riding around without the registration," Jed volunteered.

She gave him a look that shot daggers. "Stop *helping* me," she growled, then looked back at the patrolman with a falsely happy smile. "I won the Crystal Cove Merchants' Harvest Bonanza Grand Giveaway. The prize was this car. We were trying it out, but I'm afraid Mr. Carrow forgot to tell me where the registration is. Uh, maybe it's not in my name yet, but—"

"You won the car?" Al Gresham asked excitedly. He lifted his camera. "I've got to get a few shots of this. It'll make great copy for next Wednesday's paper. 'The winner of the car celebrates by getting a ticket.'"

Caitlin's heart stopped. She held up both hands. "No, please," she whimpered.

Jed looked at her and finally began to clue in to her distress. "Hey, Al, you don't want to do that."

Too late. Caitlin threw her hands out to stop what was about to happen, but the newspaperman began snapping pictures. She heard the shutter click at least six times.

"No," she said. "Don't. Please don't print that."

Jed started after Al, but the man skipped back to the patrol car, jumped inside and locked the doors. "Al, you always were a damned jerk," Jed said, rattling the door handle and pounding the flat of his hand against the window. Al held up the camera and grinned, which infuriated Jed even more.

While Jed was yelling at Al, the patrolman seemed to take pity on Caitlin. No doubt he was more concerned about the possibility of a homicide, so he gave her a speech about safe driving and always carrying her registration, then let her off with a warning, which she signed and accepted with shaking fingers. Fervently she promised to get the registration form right away and always keep it in the car.

Jed stalked back to her as Brentanski returned to the

patrol car and Al unlocked the door for him. Caitlin was grateful that the policeman seemed to have forgotten about the Breathalyzer test. No doubt Al would have wanted to photograph that, too. She was grateful when another car zoomed by, catching Brent's attention. The officer started the patrol car, switched off his blinking lights and followed the other vehicle.

"Are you all right?" Jed asked when they were alone.

Caitlin threw up her hands. "My whole professional life in Crystal Cove flashed before my eyes, but oh, yes, I'm just dandy. No thanks to you," she tacked on. Furiously she whipped around, forgetting about the pothole by her car door. She stumbled and snapped the heel off her other pump.

"Aaargh!" Bending down, she grabbed the heel and threw it across the highway, then took off both her shoes and sent them sailing, too.

"Aw, Caitlin, it's not that bad," Jed said, standing by her door.

She pushed him out of the way, jerked open the door and fell inside. The finger she pointed at him shook with rage. "You kissed me for an advertisement on the *Midnight Movie*. You twisted my arm to take you for a ride where you encouraged me to speed—"

"Oh, come on," he said, growing angry, too. "That was your decision."

"Yes, it was, fool that I am. I don't know why I ever listened to you. You almost got me a ticket, nearly got me having to take a Breathalyzer—"

"Hey, that wasn't my fault. You were the one who fell out of the car like a sailor after a three-day shore leave."

She was too furious to be deterred. Waving away his objections, she said, "You almost let them think I'd stolen this car, and then you couldn't keep your mouth shut so that Mr. Happy Snappy took my picture for the paper."

"I tried to get it away from him," he pointed out.

"If you hadn't said anything, it wouldn't have been necessary."

"Oh, for crying out loud, Cait, he was looking for something to photograph. That's why he was out with Brent tonight. That's why he had his camera in his hands. He would have taken your picture, anyway. Besides, everyone knows they never get anything right in that paper, and—"

"That's not the point!"

"Caitlin, you're not being logical."

"Logic has no place here or I wouldn't be out on this highway with you!" she yelled.

Jed must have realized he'd said the wrong thing because he held up his hands placatingly. "All right, forget that. I don't understand why you're so mad about me kissing you in a TV advertisement and about your picture being taken for the paper."

"Because I'm *trying* to build a professional reputation in this town." Her hands were still trembling, but she reached down and started the engine.

"A couple of incidents like this won't affect that." Jed stalked around the car and reached for the door handle. "People know you're trustworthy. You're overreacting."

That was too much. Caitlin hit the accelerator and the tires spat gravel as the car lurched ahead.

"Hey, Caitlin. Stop!" Jed shouted. His hand was on the door handle. He held on to it as he sprinted to keep up.

"No!" she hollered back, but she had to pause as she pulled off the shoulder and onto the roadway. When she did so, Jed slapped both hands down on the door frame and dove inside headfirst as she accelerated.

Jed landed with his head almost in her lap and his feet dangling out the window. He'd banged his elbow on the door frame, but at least he was inside the car. He looked up at Caitlin's face and decided instantly that he had never seen an angrier woman. Logic hadn't worked in trying to calm her down. Maybe he should try charm.

She glanced down at him and swiped an elbow at his head. He ducked away from her. "Sit up straight," she ordered. "With your feet hanging out like that, people will think I've got a dead body in here."

As they entered the Crystal Cove city limits, the streetlights illuminated her face. Jed examined the murderous look in her eyes as he sat up, rubbing his elbow. "They wouldn't be far wrong," he muttered.

She ignored him.

"Caitlin, you worry too much about what people will think," Jed goaded her.

"I have to, Jed, if I'm going to be successful."

"Your success doesn't depend on a couple of incidents like this. It's built day by day, like you've been doing since you moved here."

"A couple of incidents like this won't help."

Jed rubbed his hand across his face to see if the coldness in her tone had frost forming on his eyebrows. He opened his mouth to tell her to calm down, but then he snapped it shut. She *was* calm. Icily so, and it alarmed him. Icy indifference was the last thing he wanted from her. He tried again. "Caitlin, your clients or potential clients who see the TV advertisement or the picture in the paper will think you're a good sport."

She threw him another angry glance, but she didn't answer. He gave up trying to convince her.

They reached the house a few minutes later and Caitlin pulled to a stop. As they climbed out of the car, Jed decided it would be in his best interests to apologize. Though he'd only been trying to help, things had gone badly wrong—at least in her eyes.

He strolled around the front of the car as she carefully locked the doors and said, "Thanks for taking me for a ride, Caitlin. I'm sorry you got stopped."

She flicked a glance at him. "I'm sorry I listened to you. I think I'm the one who got taken for a ride."

"Oh, come on, Caitlin!" Jed exclaimed, losing his patience with her single-minded stubbornness. "You're overreacting. Sure some people will see the TV ad and—"

"And *everybody* will see the newspaper."

"But who's going to care?"

"Me!" Caitlin jabbed a thumb at her chest.

Jed balled his hands into fists and punched them down to his sides. "Why won't you listen to me? This isn't going to harm you professionally. The people who know you will be glad for your good fortune. Those who don't will be envious, but so what? Either way, it will mean free publicity."

"Not the kind I want!" Caitlin took a deep breath and clutched her hands together so hard her knuckles were white.

Jed shook his head, breathed a gusty sigh and muttered, "I should have wrestled that camera away from Al, the little twerp. Maybe I'll raise his rent."

Caitlin frowned at him. "Raise his rent?"

"I own the *Clarion* building."

Caitlin stared at him as an admittedly crazy thought formed in her head. "Jed," she said slowly, "if you own the building, that means you have a key."

"Sure," he shrugged. "Why?"

"Because if you've got a key you can get into the *Clarion* office."

"Why would I want to...?" He gaped at her. "You want me to break in and get those pictures?"

Caitlin nodded vigorously. "Don't you see that's the best solution?"

"It's breaking and entering!"

"Not if you've got the key."

"I've got the key, but I've also got a rental agreement in which I promise not to come into their offices unless it's an emergency."

"Well, what do you think this is?" she demanded.

"This is hardly a threat to life and limb."

Caitlin glared at him. "That shows how much you know," she said grimly. She looked down at his legs as if trying to decide which one to break first.

He gave her a wild look. "Aren't you the one who was worrying about risking your professional reputation? How would it look if we broke in and got caught?"

"*We?*"

"You don't think I'm going to do this *alone*, do you?"

"Does that mean you'll do it, then?" she asked eagerly, jumping on the part she wanted to hear.

Jed opened his mouth and she was sure he was going to refuse, but then his head tilted back and he assessed her with a calculating gleam in his eyes. "On a couple of conditions."

Warily she asked, "What conditions?"

"I'll let you know after we finish at the *Clarion* office."

"There you go with that 'we' again."

"That's one of the conditions. If I do this, you're coming with me."

She held up her hands. "Wait, wait, wait. I'm not going to agree unless I know what the other conditions are."

"You don't have any choice," he said smugly. "You need me to do this for you, so you have to do something for me. It's a one-time offer. Take it or leave it."

She really didn't like the way this was headed. She rubbed her knuckles across her forehead. "Oh, Jed—"

"Take it or leave it," he repeated. "And we'll shake on it." He stuck out his hand.

Reluctantly Caitlin looked at him, then down at his hand. This was a risk. She didn't like risks. Every one she'd taken with him had shaken her up. Still, the thought of her picture in the paper getting a speeding ticket was a risk, too. Maybe, as Jed had said, she was overreacting, but this was a small town, and she had to think of her image.

"Oh, quit looking like I'm trying to hand you a live grenade," Jed groused. "This is a straightforward business deal. I do something for you. You do something for me."

Her bottom lip thrust out as she thought it over. "Why do I have the feeling this isn't as cut and dried as you're making it sound?"

"Because for some reason I have yet to figure out, you've talked yourself into thinking I'm the bad guy."

"I never said you were."

"Oh, forget it," he said, dropping the hand he'd been holding out. "Trust me. I'm not going to do anything to hurt you."

Where had she heard that before? Caitlin wondered. Oh, yes. How could she have forgotten? He'd whispered those words to her when he'd taken her to bed. She had believed him then, been enthralled and touched by his tenderness. He hadn't hurt her. He'd treated her with all the care his words had promised.

Caitlin put a stop to those thoughts and could almost hear the brakes screeching in her brain. She was getting way off track. He was right. He hadn't done anything to hurt her then and he wouldn't now. He'd never pretended to be anything except what he was, an outgoing, friendly guy who made no promises. *She* was the one who'd made that night into something it wasn't.

Drawing a steadying breath, she reached out, grabbed his hand and gave it a quick, sharp shake. "It's a deal. Let's go." She whirled back toward her new car.

If he was surprised by her sudden capitulation, he didn't show it. Instead, he called out, "Wait, Caitlin. You need to change your clothes."

Ruefully she glanced down at the bare toes sticking through her shredded stockings. "Oh, yes, I may need shoes."

"Not only shoes. You need to change all your clothes. Do you have anything dark?"

"Dark?"

"We're breaking and entering, remember? We've got to be dressed right."

"Well, I have some black leggings and a sweatshirt," she said.

"Perfect. How about a black cap?"

"Maybe." She frowned at him. "Shall I see if I can find a stick of night camouflage makeup?"

"Have you got one?" he asked hopefully.

"No."

"Well, maybe we can smear some mud on our faces," he suggested.

"Are you kidding?"

"Wait and see. Let's go get changed." He shooed her

into the house, up the stairs and into her apartment. "Make it quick," he said, leaving her at her door.

As instructed, Caitlin scrambled into her leggings, sweatshirt and black sneakers. Because the outfit had no pockets, she hooked a fanny pack around her waist, then placed a small flashlight and her keys inside.

She wasn't sure why she had to go through all this simply to stroll into a building that Jed actually owned, but she had told herself she was going to trust him and she was anxious to keep those awful pictures of her from being published. As she dressed, excitement ran through her. She had never done anything like this before. When she met Jed in the hallway, she saw that he was dressed in a similar outfit, though his sweater was navy blue.

She gave it a close look. The hem sagged, the neck was too wide, there were several dropped stitches right in the center of his chest, and loose ends of yarn stuck out here and there. Besides these charming features, it was big enough for two people to crawl inside and have a picnic. "Nice sweater," she said, trying to keep the humor out of her voice. "Did it come with its own tent pole?"

"It is a little big," Jed admitted. "Suzy Briscoe knitted it for me." He stretched his arms out in front of him and put his wrists together. "If I keep the sleeves pushed up, you can't even tell that one sleeve is two inches longer than the other."

Caitlin dipped her chin so he couldn't see the laughter in her eyes. "Is this her first attempt at knitting?"

"Nah. I've got three more of these, but this is the only dark one." He gave her an innocent smile. "Suzy feels bad because she dumped me last year for Dan Welby."

"Are you sure you didn't dump her and this is her revenge?" Caitlin asked. Somehow she couldn't resist some gentle jabs at him and at Suzy's sweater, but she didn't understand the nip of jealousy she felt.

"You don't like it?"

"It's fine," she said. "Precisely what you need for a little breaking and entering." She grasped his arm and started for the stairs. "Let's go. What are you going to do, by the way?"

"I figure Brent's shift probably ended at ten. He would have dropped Al by the *Clarion* office and Al would have left the camera there and gone home."

"What makes you think Al didn't go home and take the camera with him?"

"Because he's an obsessive-compulsive little creep who likes everything in its place, including his camera."

"Sounds like you know him."

"We went to school together. He used to keep his pens and pencils in neat little rows in his desk," Jed said in disgust. "He charged daily rental to anyone who borrowed one from him, with an extra ten cents added if you chewed it, sharpened it too much or wore it down and *forgot* to sharpen it."

Caitlin squinted at him skeptically. "That can't be true."

"Why would I lie?" Jed asked. "I used to save his butt when the other guys beat up on him. I'm beginning to regret that."

Caitlin grinned. "So what's your plan for getting the film back?"

"We'll wait around outside the *Clarion* building to see if Al is coming back. If he doesn't, we'll know he's already been there. Then we'll go inside, get the camera and retrieve the film."

Her eyes widened. "That's it? Walk in the front door and get the film. That's your plan?"

He flashed his riverboat-gambler's grin. "Well, the back door actually, but yeah, that's pretty much the plan."

"I thought you said you didn't want to do this because we would be breaking and entering."

"We'll be in an office we have no right to be in. That's bad enough."

Caitlin skidded to a stop. "And for that, we needed dark clothing?"

"Not really," he answered, his grin growing wicked. "I wanted to see you in a pair of leggings." He glanced down at her slim legs. "Nice," he said appreciatively. "I've got a thing for leggings. Tights, too. Someone should have thought of shrink-wrapping women's legs years ago."

Caitlin gave him a sharp look. "I'd love to know what goes on inside your head."

He wiggled his eyebrows comically and leered at her. "Honey, I think you already know. Besides, you would have frozen in that dress, and…"

When his voice trailed off, Caitlin stopped on the stairs and turned around. "What?"

His glance darted around the stairway as he avoided her gaze. "I didn't like the way Brent and Al were looking at you."

Was that jealousy she heard? In spite of herself, she was delighted. "How were they looking at me?"

"Like you were a safe-deposit box and they had the only key."

With a laugh, Caitlin preceded him through the front door, then waited while he locked it. When she headed for her new car, he pulled her back. "We'll go in mine. If Al is around he might see yours and remember it because it's so noticeable."

Caitlin glanced at Jed's golden-yellow Mustang. "And yours isn't?"

"At least he hasn't seen it in the glare of rotating bubble lights." He slanted her a sheepish look. "Well, at least not recently. Maybe he won't remember who it belongs to."

Resisting the urge to remind him that it was probably the only car in town that had broken all known land-speed records, she climbed inside, fastened the seat belt and tightened it.

Amused, Jed watched her. "Don't cut off the circulation to your legs," he warned. "You might not be able to run if we need to make a quick getaway from the cops."

Caitlin braced herself as they took off like a cannon shot. "Then you'll have to carry me."

5

WITHIN MOMENTS, THEY WERE cruising through Crystal Cove. Jed turned into the parking lot behind the building that housed the *Clarion* and wedged the Mustang into the farthest corner, behind the Dumpster. "In case someone sees it from the street," he whispered, glancing around furtively. There were no lights on in the building. They waited for several minutes, but saw no one. Jed checked the glowing dial of his watch. "It's after ten. Al's probably already been here. Let's go get that film."

They exited the car quickly, but nearly dove back inside when they heard a rustling noise in the Dumpster, then relaxed with a sigh of relief as a cat appeared briefly on top, spied them and ducked back inside. Jed and Caitlin took a couple of deep breaths to steady their nerves.

"Probably one of Mrs. Zachary's cats," Jed whispered. "She's got about a hundred of them living with her in that house across the alley and they're all as mean as she is."

Caitlin nodded and pummeled her heart back down into place.

They scurried across the parking lot, gazes sweeping the area and the alley behind to make sure they were unobserved and no more cats were going to leap out at them. They had a few nervous moments when they reached the well-lit back door and Jed's key didn't seem to fit, but then it turned and they were inside. Jed quickly punched in the code for the alarm system, and they both gulped for oxygen.

"Now I know why I didn't want to do this," Caitlin said. "I don't have the nerve for it."

"Relax. All we have to do is see if Al brought the camera back, find out if the film is in it, take it and get out of here." He took a flashlight from his pocket, covered the beam with his fingers so that only a small amount of light came through, then carefully played the light around the back hallway.

"Piece of cake," Caitlin agreed, though she wasn't too sure. "Won't Al notice there's no film in the camera? And how do we know we'll get the right roll of film?"

"I doubt he'd have used more than one roll. There's not that much happening in Crystal Cove on a Friday night—which is why he was so hot to get your picture."

"How fortunate that I get to be the featured attraction on a slow news day."

Jed chuckled, then he pulled her close and spoke in her ear. "Get behind me," he urged, "and stay close."

"Is that really necessary?" she asked, fully aware that the brush of his breath against her ear was causing wildly erotic thoughts to blossom.

"Nah, I've just always wanted to say that."

She rolled her eyes, but did as he said, moving close behind him. Trust Jed Bishop to turn breaking and entering into a game. They moved down the hallway to a large room where a row of desks stood. Caitlin had been in here before when she'd placed an ad announcing the opening of her office, but she hadn't paid much attention to the layout. "Where's Al's office?"

Keeping her close behind him by reaching around and placing his hand at her waist, Jed used his other hand to shine a tiny beam of light around the room. "It used to be the one on the right, but it looks like they've rearranged things. We'll have to look around."

Caitlin unzipped her fanny pack and pulled out her own small flashlight, then zipped it shut again. "We'd better split up to search or we'll be here all night."

"Okay. You go to the left. I'll go to the right. We're sure to find it."

"Got it." Cautiously they moved away from each other. She knew it was silly, but without Jed's presence, her stomach felt jittery. Turning away to the left, she felt a tug on her fanny pack and reached down to adjust it. She headed for the first open door on the left, which loomed like a dark cavern. She'd only taken a few steps when she heard something topple over.

"Jed, what was that?"

"I didn't hear anything."

Sure her overactive imagination was playing tricks on her, she frowned. They'd better find that film fast and get out of here before her imagination really went into overdrive. She took a few more steps and heard several more things fall.

"Jed, you can't tell me you didn't hear that." She swung her flashlight toward him. "You knocked something over."

"I did not," he insisted. "I'm standing in the center of the room."

"Well, be careful, anyway."

They had each taken a few more steps when they heard more things hitting the floor. Caitlin spun around. Even more crashes and thumps. "Jed! What are you *doing?*"

"Not a damned thing. What are *you* doing?" He swung his flashlight around to her face.

Caitlin blinked when the narrow beam hit her in the

eyes. "I'm *trying* to find Al's office, but you keep knocking things over."

"*Me?* I haven't touched a thing."

"Well, stop it," she said, exasperated. He made a rude noise at her. They both turned away, heading in opposite directions. This time she heard the distinctive sound of a pencil holder hitting the floor, spraying its contents across the tile, then there was another muffled thump, and she was brought up short by something tugging on her fanny pack again. "What in the world...?" She reached for the fanny pack and pointed the flashlight at it. A long string of yarn extended from the zipper and off into the darkness. She followed it with the beam of her flashlight across the room, over three desks whose tops were a shambles, to the back of Jed's head.

"Hey," she said. "Look."

He whipped around, pulling the thread taut and sweeping the surface of another desk. A framed photograph clattered to the floor, followed by a lightweight tape dispenser. A top-heavy halogen lamp wobbled on the edge of the desk, and Jed made a lunge for it, scooting it back barely in time. Dumbfounded, he stared at her.

"It's your sweater," she said frantically. "A loose end on the back caught in the zipper of my fanny pack. It's unraveled and knocked over everything between us."

"Well, then, come here," Jed growled. He reached behind his back, snagged the thread and began reeling her in.

"Wait," she called out. "Let me unzip..." Too late. Jed's hard tug on the yarn pulled her across the floor, she hit the corner of a desk and sprawled across it, clearing the top with her outspread arms. Her elbow hit the corner of a computer monitor, and she had to scramble to grab it and keep it from toppling over the edge.

Jed was beside her in a second, helping her stand, pulling the loose yarn from the zipper. With a tangle of crumpled-up yarn and his flashlight in one hand and his other hand wrapped around her arm, he turned her so they could survey the damage. The area around them was a shambles.

"Oh, great," he murmured. "We've got to clean this up."

"How will we know what goes where?" Caitlin asked, bending to grab a handful of items from the floor.

"We don't. We'll have to—" He spun around. "What was that?"

She shot to her feet when she heard the slam of a car door. "Someone's coming!"

They whirled toward the front windows. A patrol car could be seen pulling away from the curb. "It's Al," Jed said. "Brent's dropped him off."

"I thought you said—"

"How was I supposed to know the two of them would be late? They probably stopped off for coffee and doughnuts."

"Let's get out of here." Leaving behind the mess they'd made, they sprinted for the back of the building. "Do you think he'll know we've been here?" she asked.

"He'll know *somebody's* been here. And even Al's smart enough to think it was us." Jed shot back. "I've got a key, remember? And he knows we don't want those pictures published. He might figure out we were trying to get our hands on the film."

They whipped the back door open and tumbled out. A loud shriek had them jumping out of their skins. They both looked down at a squirming black-and-white ball of fur.

"Mrs. Zachary's cat," Caitlin said, nearly hyperventilating in her fright. His tail was caught under Jed's foot. He lashed around wildly. "Is he okay?"

Thinking fast, Jed bent down and scooped the animal up, grunting in pain when claws made contact with his unprotected hands. He examined the feline quickly. "Yeah. Spitting mad, but okay." He bent to put the cat down. "Let's get— Hey, I know what to do." Turning, he tossed the cat inside the back door, then closed it and locked it.

Caitlin gaped at him. "What did you do that for?"

"Al will think the cat got inside somehow and did all that damage and that one of his staff left the alarm off. We'll be in the clear." He grabbed Caitlin's arm and sprinted for the car. "But we'd be smart to get the hell out of here."

Caitlin didn't bother to respond. He was right, but they had failed in their mission. Her unflattering picture was going to appear in the paper. Still, that was better than lining up for a mug shot at the police station. She gripped Jed's hand and ran.

Jed and Caitlin didn't stop running until they reached the car. They crept out of the parking lot, with their lights off, coasted by the front windows, where they could see Al darting wildly around the brightly lit room. He was waving his arms, yelling and attempting an Irish jig.

"I guess he found the cat," Jed said in a mild tone.

Caitlin, high on adrenaline, answered with a wild giggle.

"I'm no expert at lipreading, but I never would have guessed Al knew so many four-letter words or that he knew how to dance like that," Jed said.

Once they were beyond the building, Jed flipped on the headlights, stepped on the gas and raced for home. He noticed that, for once, Caitlin didn't complain about the speed of his driving. She was as glad to get away from there as he was. When they reached home, they rushed in their front door and slammed it shut.

Still shivering from fright, Caitlin waited on the stairs while he locked the door behind them and then joined her.

"What do you think happened when Al got hold of that cat?" she asked, her golden-brown eyes sparkling wickedly.

With a grin, Jed placed his hand on the railing and nodded toward it. "Probably the same thing that happened to me."

Caitlin looked down and gasped at the raw, red scratches on his hands. One was deep enough to have drawn dots of blood along its length "Oh, Jed," she said, horrified. "Why didn't you say something?"

"What would have been the point? I don't have a first-aid kit in the car, and besides, I was busy making our getaway."

"Come into my apartment," she said, taking his arm and tugging upward with a gentle touch as if he'd suddenly become an invalid. "I've got some antiseptic cream we can put on the scratches. You don't think those will leave scars, do you?"

Jed almost said he could take care of the scratches himself, but then told himself not to be a fool. This was the first time Caitlin had shown such solicitous concern for him. He should milk it for all it was worth. He would need all the sympathy he could garner when he sprung the second half of their agreement on her.

"I guess we'll have to wait and see," he said in a long-suffering tone.

His lips pinched together as if he was stifling the pain. He'd seen Steve Martin do that in a movie, and it had worked up sympathy from the female lead pretty effectively.

Caitlin ushered him into her apartment, had him sit on the couch, then bustled around finding cotton balls, hydrogen peroxide and antiseptic cream. He sat back, enjoying himself, and decided he didn't mind this at all. When she bent over to lay the items out on the coffee table, he had a nice view of her sweetly rounded bottom. He would have given it a little pat if he hadn't known she'd turn around and belt him. It was pleasant to have a woman fussing over him, though he admitted he'd had more than his share of it in his life. Even though he was one of four, he'd been pampered. When he'd moved out on his own, he'd discovered there were plenty of women who liked doing things for him. That was okay, because he'd done things for them, too. He'd fixed their cars or their roofs, dragged their cats out of trees. Caitlin was the first woman he'd been with—short-lived though it had been—who didn't want him to do anything for her.

Funny, it hadn't occurred to him sooner to have *her* do something for *him*. She was a nurturing, caring person with all the little old ladies whose finances she handled. It was only him she kept at a distance, but he thought the experiences they'd shared tonight might go a ways toward changing that.

He held out his hands when she ordered him to and watched as her slim, efficient fingers dabbed hydrogen peroxide on the scratches.

His breath hissed in. "Ouch!"

She winced in sympathy and gave him a melting look. "I'm sorry. I didn't think it would sting so much."

He lifted his chin. "I'm strong. I can take it."

She giggled again as she dabbed on the antiseptic cream. It was a sound he'd never heard her make before tonight and he liked it. He never would have suspected she was a giggling kind of woman. "There," she said, capping the tube and laying it aside. "That should take care of it."

"Thanks," Jed said. He looked around. "I don't suppose you'd let me have a beer, would you?"

"Why not? You paid for them." She brought him one, then sat in the chair opposite him. That wasn't good. He wanted her nearby.

He was considering telling her that and working the sympathy angle when she looked up and said, "I really appreciate what you tried to do tonight, Jed. Getting the film back, I mean."

"Too bad we didn't succeed. I'll talk to Al again tomorrow and see what I can do, but this is Friday, and the paper goes to the printer tomorrow, so it may already be too late."

She grimaced. "I know."

"Listen, Cait—"

She held up her hand to stop him. "Don't tell me again that it won't affect my reputation in this town. I'm not ready to hear that." She frowned at the floor for a moment, then glanced up. "We had an agreement and I'm willing to honor it. What is it I'm supposed to do for you?"

Dread settled in Jed's stomach. He took a sip of his beer. "Well," he began slowly, "it's part of the Harvest Bonanza celebration...."

He let his voice trail off. It sounded so silly and he didn't know why he'd let himself get talked into it again this year. Caitlin nodded, her earnest face encouraging him to go on.

Jed gulped in a deep breath, expelled it, then took a sip of his beer as he mumbled something.

Caitlin leaned closer. "What did you say? A bachelor, what?"

"Auction," he mumbled again, swallowing more beer. He felt color climbing his cheeks in a blush. Gad, when was the last time he'd done that?

"You're kidding." She sat back and stared at him.

"Nope. They've done it every other year for ten years. I think it's way outlived its time, but the women in town seem to like it, and there's usually a few new bachelors in town who get roped into it."

"And this year, you're one of them?"

"Yeah. I've managed to duck it most years by being out of town, driving for Steve, but my mother threatened to disinherit me if I skipped it this year. The women's club puts it on and she's the current women's club president. They use the money to buy books for the school libraries."

"Oh, well, it's for a good cause, then," Caitlin said, sitting back and looking at him with teasing enjoyment in her eyes.

Jed frowned. "I'm not one of those who believes the old 'anything for a good cause' routine,' especially after what happened two years ago."

Caitlin sat forward eagerly. "Why? What happened?"

Steeling himself to face the memory, Jed said, "The Carlton twins bought me and my promised date of an evening on the town in San Francisco."

"That sounds like fun, but..." Caitlin paused, her gaze going inward for a second, then her eyes widened. "The Carlton twins. The two ladies who bring you jam."

"And crocheted booties."

"I think they're supposed to be slippers."

"With pom-poms on the toes?" Jed asked, horrified. "Baby-blue ones?"

"I've never seen you wear them," Caitlin pointed out, her sympathy lost in a wave of amusement.

"I don't. I use them to polish my car."

"And this all started with the bachelor auction two years ago?"

"Well, no. I'd been in the bachelor auction before and they'd bought me each time. It was sort of a tradition."

Caitlin thought about the other females who visited his apartment. "Didn't any *younger* women get to bet on you?"

"They tried, but Edith and Evelyn intimidated them into giving up by glaring at them. There may have been voodoo dolls involved, too, but I'm not sure." He winced. "Probably crocheted ones."

She tried to picture it and failed. "So you've been on more than one date with them?"

"Three. The first two weren't too bad, but the third was...bleak."

"That's too bad," she said sympathetically. "I understand that the bachelor auction must be a community-wide affair and all, but isn't it a little strange for them to want a date with you? I mean, they're a little old for you, aren't they?"

He nodded sorrowfully. "They don't look their age, what with the red hair color, blue eye shadow, gold spandex pants and sequins, but yeah, they're in their seventies."

In spite of her sympathy for him, Caitlin erupted into laughter. He gave her a disgruntled look. "You wouldn't have thought it was so funny if you'd been there. Edith, who is definitely the dominant twin, forgot her hearing aids, so I had to bellow at her all evening. When she doesn't have her hearing aids, she tends to shout, as well, so everyone in the restaurant heard her yelling that she had to have stewed prunes every day or she couldn't—"

"I get the picture," Caitlin said, holding up her hand and laughing even harder.

"Well, good, because I didn't want to have to spell it out. All that was bad enough, but then Evelyn's dentures broke, the top plate split right down the middle, so she couldn't eat anything. She took the thing out and waved it around for all to see while Edith screamed at her to put the damned thing back in her mouth."

"Oh, no!" Weak with laughter, Caitlin was sitting back on the chair, holding her sides. "What ha...happened?"

"Well, the date ended early, real early, and we started home. Evelyn sat up front with me on the way to the city, and Edith was supposed to sit up front on the way home, but Evelyn said she'd be carsick if she had to sit in the back since she hadn't had any dinner."

"Because of the broken dentures."

"Right." Jed nodded and sipped his beer, trying not to shudder at the memory. "So Edith refused and the two of them got into an argument right there in the parking lot, Edith saying Evelyn always got her own way because she was older by ten minutes and Evelyn saying—" He broke off. "Well, actually, I don't know what Evelyn was saying because I couldn't understand her."

"Because of the broken denture," Caitlin said again, choking with laughter.

"Yeah. Anyway, we finally got home with both of them sitting in the front bucket seat, jabbing each other in the ribs, and I swore not to be part of that auction again."

He watched as Caitlin sat up and fumbled for a tissue in the box by her chair. She swiped tears from her eyes. He had never seen her laugh so hard. Seeing her like this caused a fist of desire to curl itself up and punch him right in the stomach. He set his beer down and licked his lips. He could imagine kissing that soft, giving mouth of hers. The one taste he'd had this evening, hours ago now, hadn't been nearly enough. He wondered if there was some way to maneuver her into another one.

"Jed, how do you get yourself into these things?"

"Luck of the draw." He shrugged.

"There's got to be more to it than that."

He should have known she wouldn't accept an easy answer. He took another swallow of beer, then rubbed his hand over his jaw. "You know I like to help people," he said finally.

"Oh, yes," she answered, lifting an eyebrow at him. Obviously she was recalling the incident with Brent and Al.

"It's kind of a lifelong thing. My sister Diana is diabetic, and since I'm a year older, I always kind of looked out for her. After she grew up and left home, I guess I expanded my helpfulness to other people."

"Whether they want it or not," she added dryly.

"Hey," he protested, "you'd be surprised how many people can't make plans and decisions on their own and want a little help and advice. Besides, it usually works out for the best—with a few minor adjustments."

Caitlin chuckled. "So, how did you let yourself get talked into this bachelor auction again if you swore not to?" she asked.

"My mom signed me up and then told me about it. I kept thinking I could get out of it, but so far, no deal. That's where you come in."

She gave him a cautious look. "Me?"

"Yeah, I want you to buy me."

"You do? Why?"

"Because then I'll know I'm being bought by someone who's at least relatively normal."

"Thanks a lot!"

"You know what I mean. Edith and Evelyn don't have any real romantic interest in me. It's only that they're so competitive with each other. They get tired of each other's company and they get lonely. Somehow they've convinced themselves that I'm bored and need their help. They don't want me to be lonely."

Caitlin's mouth dropped open. "*You?* Women march through your place like General Sherman's troops through the South."

Jed's eyes widened and he sat up straight, staring at her. What was this? he thought. His smile morphed into a knowing grin. "Oh, yeah?" he said. "You've been keeping track of my visitors?"

She lifted her chin. "Certainly not. I happened to notice. In a purely casual way, of course."

He chuckled. "Of course."

"Now go on with what you were saying," she instructed. "The Carltons think you're lonely…"

"And bored. They have a thing against being bored. They think it's a deadly disease, so they try to liven up my life."

"Sounds like they've succeeded."

"No kidding." Jed sat forward and gave her a pleading look. "Come on, Cait, you don't want to see me on another date from hell with the glitter twins, do you?" When she grinned, he said, "Don't answer that!"

Caitlin tilted her head and pursed her lips as she thought it over. He *really* wished she wouldn't do that. "Well, I do owe you for trying to get that film back."

"Good. I'll give you the money to buy me. Remember

you've got to outbid everybody and don't let any audience mutterings about respect for old age get to you."

"I understand. But Jed, you've got so many girlfriends, couldn't one of them…?"

"I've got lots of *friends* who are women, but most of them are involved with someone. Besides, you're the one who owes me a favor."

"I see," she said, then gave a long-suffering sigh. "All right. I'll do it, and I'll be stalwart no matter how many little old ladies threaten me with canes and false teeth."

"Hold that thought." Jed let his eyes drift partly shut and gave Caitlin a sly look from beneath his lashes. "You do understand, though, that you'll then be committed to an actual date with me?"

She blinked. Obviously that hadn't occurred to her. Slowly she put her hands on her hips. "I don't think so, Bishop."

He leaned forward and met her gaze. "I know so, Ms. Beck. After all, you're very concerned about your reputation. How would it look if you backed out of an agreement?"

Caitlin's mouth opened and closed a couple of times. He had her and they both knew it. Before he lost his advantage, Jed stood up and moved toward the door. "See you," he said.

Caitlin bounced out of her chair and dashed after him. "Wait a minute, Jed."

"Can't," he said, swinging open the door. "Gotta go."

She whirled in front of him and slammed it shut. "It's one thing to help you out, but—"

Since he didn't like the direction that statement was heading, Jed shut her up in the best way he knew how. He kissed her.

He meant for it to be casual, light, a teasing way to

head off her arguments. Instead, the instant their lips touched, it became sweet and tender. He wanted her, but if she knew how much, it would scare her off yet again, and he didn't want that to happen, so he tasted and tempted her, wooing her with the touch of his lips and tongue.

Caitlin's lips trembled open, accepting what he offered. Her hands clasped his upper arms as if she wanted to push him away, then they moved up and over his shoulders, blazing a heat trail in their wake. Jed made a low, growling sound in his throat and reached out to wrap his arms around her and hold her close as he tilted her head back to deepen the kiss.

Damn, he thought dizzily, damn, he'd missed this. One night with her hadn't been enough. A thousand might not be enough. This wasn't the way it was supposed to be, he thought hazily. He loved women, but liked things free and easy, loose, mutually satisfying and temporary. This didn't feel temporary. He pulled back and stared down into her eyes which had gone deep gold with desire. He'd done that to her, he thought with a wild moment of triumph. He'd made her feel that level of passion. The look in her eyes almost caused him to drag her back to finish what he'd started, but somehow better sense prevailed. He carefully set her away from him, then moved her from where she blocked the door.

"Good night, Cait," he said. "Remember our agreement."

She nodded as if her head was attached to a spring, then her face clouded. "Agreement?"

Before she could remember, and before that dazed, sexy look on her face got to him, he scooted out the door and across the hall.

JED ARRIVED AT Caitlin's office the next morning carrying coffee and doughnuts. He set them on her desk as she turned away from her computer and greeted him with a surprised look. He twirled a straight-backed chair around and pulled it up to the edge of the desk, then sat, straddling it backward.

"It's Saturday, Caitlin," he said. "Why are you working?"

Caitlin removed her reading glasses, laid them on the desk, then took a deep breath. The morning was cool and, along with the coffee aroma, he'd brought the scent of fresh ocean air in with him.

Easy, girl, Caitlin thought as her heart fluttered. She had relived his kisses a hundred times last night, had dreamed about him all night and here he was in the flesh.

She'd thought she could escape by coming to work, but he'd followed her. She felt her heart soften. How lucky could a girl get? "I have a few things to do," she said.

"You work too hard."

"That's what Eunice tells me." Eunice Grandy came in several hours a week to help Caitlin out with secretarial duties. She was a whiz at keeping the office organized, and Caitlin planned to hire her full-time as soon as she could afford it.

"I've been to the *Clarion* office," he announced.

"Have you?" Caitlin picked up a doughnut and took a delicate bite.

"Lots of talk over there about a mysterious cat that somehow got inside and wrecked the place."

"No!"

He pulled his face into a long, serious frown. "It's true. Al found the cat still inside the office last night. It was quite a battle to get it outside again."

Caitlin sipped her coffee, though she thought she might

choke on rising laughter, and viewed him over the rim of the paper cup. "Who won the battle?"

"From the scratches on Al's face, I'd say the cat won."

"Oh?"

"Yeah. Al said the cat stood about two feet high and weighed fifty pounds."

"Hefty cat."

"Or an average-size bobcat."

"Are they native to this area?"

"This is the first I've heard of one," Jed said, grinning, delighting in their shared secret. "Poor Al had to use a whip and a chair to get the monster out the door."

"Brave man."

The two of them looked at each other and burst out laughing. It took them several minutes to calm down. Finally Caitlin drew in a shaky breath and said, "What about the photos?"

"He won't budge, says the public has a right to see them, that the car you won is part of a community-wide project, blah, blah, blah."

Grimacing, Caitlin tried to stem her disappointment. "That's pretty much what he told me when I phoned him myself." No doubt the pictures would be as bad as she feared.

Jed studied her face for several seconds as he sipped his coffee. "I'm sorry," he said, startling her into looking up and meeting his eyes. The laughter they had shared was fading. "I didn't realize how much this would upset you," he went on. "Or at least, when you told me, I didn't understand."

She was so astonished she didn't know quite what to say. She stumbled around for a reply. "Oh, I see…"

"And I thought this might be a good time to talk about our partnership."

Her eyes grew wary. "What about it?"

"If you'll agree to stop trying to dissolve our partnership over the house, we can get the renovators back to work on the place. All this wrangling between us is taking up time we can't afford. Besides, now that winter is coming, we'll be having a lot of bad weather, which will delay the work even more, especially on the roof."

That sounded reasonable, though she wasn't ready to admit it. Her demand that they dissolve their partnership had been a knee-jerk reaction on her part. A reaction against the commitment she felt she'd made when she'd slept with him. She had wanted to distance herself from him, to keep from being one of the former lovers he'd turned into a friend who baked cookies for him or knitted him sweaters. It had been an immature reaction. She could see that now, and while she still wanted to be cautious, she also owed him for what he'd tried to do for her last night.

"Then what will happen when the work is done?" she asked.

He sat back and spread his hands as if he was the most easygoing and reasonable of men. "Then we'll sell the house at a tidy profit, dissolve the partnership and walk away with a nice chunk of change in our pockets."

She considered it for several seconds. "That sounds easy," she said.

"It will be easy," he said. "Then you agree to it?"

In spite of what she'd been telling herself, she was still reluctant. It meant living right across the hall from him for several more months yet. She had to be realistic and ask herself if she could resist the temptation he offered. She looked at his tousled black hair, the sexy slant of his gray eyes, the fullness of his lower lip that could kiss so devastatingly. She admired the casual way he sat with his wide shoulders at ease, his arms folded along the back of his chair, his legs splayed. Heat hopscotched up her spine. She could handle the temptation he offered.

And pigs could fly.

Jed sat forward, leaning over her desk to look into her face. "Cait, do you agree?"

"Sure." Her voice had shot up as if she'd been pinched. She cleared her throat, took another sip of coffee and repeated, "Sure."

He gave her a puzzled look and rubbed his chin. She recalled how it had felt to have that smooth jaw moving over her skin. *Focus, girl,* she told herself. *Focus.*

"All right then," Jed responded. "I'll call Appletree Construction and tell Terry Appletree to get back to work on the house. Also, I'll get Barney Mellin to tear down the old garage. There should be enough usable lumber left over for him to build a carport for your car. Maybe one for mine, too."

Pleasure flushed through her. Her hand lifted to her heart. "Why, Jed, thank you. That's so thoughtful. I don't know what to say."

"Don't say anything. From now on we'll be true partners and things will run as slick as greased glass," he said with a grin.

"That's...that's wonderful," she stammered. At last things were going to be resolved. This was what she had been wanting for weeks. Wasn't it?

He stood up quickly as if afraid she would change her mind, then grabbed his coffee and another doughnut. "I'll see you later, Caitlin. Like I said, I'll make those calls right away, then I'm going to be out of town for a couple of days. I promised Steve I'd drive a truck down to San Diego for him. Be back Monday night. Don't forget Friday is the bachelor auction."

She'd almost forgotten about that. Before she could say anything, he pointed a finger at her. "Don't try to get out of it. A promise is a promise. A deal is a deal."

"A sucker is a sucker," she responded.

With a wink and a wave, he was out the door. Caitlin turned back to work and tried to concentrate on the rows of numbers that came up on her screen. She was going to focus on work, not on how very much she was going to miss him.

6

"OF COURSE I'M NOT SAYIN' Mabel's wrong to be mad at me about this. I mean we were still teenagers when we got married. How was she supposed to know I'd turn out to be so devastatingly attractive to women?" Terry Appletree finished laying out the squares of counter tiles, then gave Caitlin an aggrieved look as he picked up his tile cutter.

"She couldn't have known, Terry. It's a burden that both of you will have to bear and share together," Caitlin answered sympathetically, pinching her lips to keep from smiling.

As promised, Jed had called both Terry and Barney Mellin to resume renovations on Monday. She had stopped by after work to see how Terry was coming with the kitchen. She was pleased to see that he had already installed the new stainless-steel sink and had begun laying the ceramic tile. She'd barely said hello before he'd begun telling her about the troubles he was having with his wife's jealousy. "The important thing is to never give her any reason to doubt you," she counseled.

He sighed and nodded his head. "You're right, but I can't help it if women look at me and find me attractive."

Caitlin made a sympathetic noise but didn't say what she was thinking—that attractiveness was in the eye of the beholder. Terry was a big man who wore slouching jeans that rode low on his hips directly under his Santa

Claus belly. He hitched them up frequently, but they always headed south again within a few seconds. He had shaggy blond hair that curled around his face, and a beatific smile that gave him a cherubic appearance. It wasn't a deceptive appearance. He wasn't very bright, but he was good-natured. He also seemed to have an unshakable belief that women lusted after him, though she'd honestly never seen any indication that he encouraged it or that this problem actually existed.

Caitlin sympathized with him because he seemed so genuinely aggrieved by this, and because he didn't use this belief to flirt with her or hit on her. Why should he? In his mind, he had enough women hungering for him already.

While Terry was working in the house, Barney Mellin, thankfully sober, was busy tearing down the old garage and sorting the wood to build a carport. Caitlin was anxious to use it for her new car. She had already found a buyer for her old one, the teenage grandson of a client. The boy wanted to fix it up. Caitlin figured the poor kid should finish that chore by the time he was a grandfather himself.

She'd been thrilled to drive her new car into town that morning, with a quick stop by Carrow Classic Cars to pick up the registration form so she could get the title changed into her name. Many people had congratulated her on her good fortune that day. She only hoped their smiles didn't turn to mocking laughter when the *Clarion* hit the stands on Wednesday.

She knew Jed was probably right—she was worrying about it too much. Of course, he didn't know she had good reason for wanting to avoid negative publicity. He knew much less about her than she knew about him. A fact he'd pointed out many times when she'd ducked his questions.

"I'll leave you alone and let you work, Terry. Call out if you need anything," Caitlin said.

"Sure thing, Ms. Beck. Hey, Jed told me you've been having trouble with your doorknob, so I took it apart and oiled it. Barney said he'd fixed it already, but he lied. Should be okay now."

"Why, thank you, Terry," she said, pleased that the problem was solved and that Jed had been so thoughtful.

He nodded his acknowledgment and switched on the radio he kept with him. As she left the room, the sounds of some new alternative rock group filled the lower floor. She was starting up the staircase when she felt a rush of cool air and turned to see two women at the open doorway.

"Hold the door," one of them said.

"*You* hold the door," the other responded. "I've got my hands full."

"And I don't?" The second one tried to elbow her way past with the result that they both got wedged in the doorway. The Carlton twins, dressed exactly alike from the hot-pink caps on their heads of flaming orange hair to their yellow spandex slacks and slick black leather boots.

Each of them held a casserole dish in her hands and had her elbows stuck out. After several jabs at each other's ribs and much jostling, wriggling and grunting, they stumbled inside.

Even if she hadn't seen them before, Caitlin would have known these were the Carlton twins by the proficiency they showed with their elbows. They stopped inside the door to exchange furious looks.

Deciding she'd better intervene before they started

throwing the casserole dishes at each other, she asked, "May I help you?"

They stopped glaring at each other and glanced up, noticing her for the first time.

"Who are you?" one of them asked.

She walked forward, smiling, to meet them in the center of the entryway. "I'm Caitlin Beck."

The two ladies exchanged a look that seemed to say, "Oh yeah?" Caitlin had seen them come to visit Jed before, but they obviously hadn't seen her. The first one drew herself up to her full five feet and gave Caitlin a stern look. "I'm Edith Carlton and this is my sister, Evelyn. We've come to see Jed Bishop."

"I'm afraid he isn't here."

"Oh? And exactly where would he be?" Evelyn asked suspiciously, shoving Edith aside so she could command Caitlin's attention.

"He's driving a truck for his brother, Steve, to San Diego. He'll probably be home tomorrow night."

"Uh-*huh*," Evelyn said, giving Caitlin a speculative look.

"I *see*," Edith chimed in. Her gaze roamed over Caitlin's russet-colored suit and matching pumps. She began to move around Caitlin in a clockwise motion, examining everything from her shiny cap of hair to her subtle gold-stud earrings. Evelyn began moving in the opposite direction, making the same survey, her casserole dish held high and away from what she obviously feared were Caitlin's prying eyes. The two women stopped before her and stood side by side, the shoulders of their identical electric blue baseball jackets brushing against each other. From beneath the brims of their pink caps, their orange bangs erupted right over their suspicious blue eyes.

"And how come you know so much about his whereabouts?" Edith asked.

"I live here, and—"

"What?" The two women straightened as if someone had jabbed them with a hot poker. They exchanged censoring looks. "You live here. With Jed?"

"Well, not—"

"What kind of young woman are you, anyway?"

Caitlin's mouth dropped open. "Excuse me?"

"Does his family know about you?" Evelyn asked.

Caitlin looked from one to the other of them. They were examining her as if she was a particularly unpleasant variety of pond scum. "Know what about me?"

Edith pinched her lips together and leaned forward. In a fierce whisper she said, "That you live with him?"

"I don't live *with* him," Caitlin said in exasperation. "I live across the hall from him in the other upstairs apartment."

"Uh-*huh*," said Evelyn again.

"I *see*," repeated Edith.

The two of them shared a look that all but screamed, *A likely story.*

"Good grief," said Caitlin in a faint voice. There was no way that she was going to convince them. Edith looked at Evelyn, who nodded knowingly.

"Well, sister," Evelyn said. "I guess we'll have to see about this."

"Yes, indeed, we will. Jed deserves better." As one, they turned and headed for the door.

Better?

"Wait," Caitlin called out, scrambling after them.

They stopped and turned. "Yes?" Their faces were grim.

"What exactly do you think is wrong with me?" Caitlin asked, lifting her hands, palms out. Did they see her as a tramp, a loose woman—what? Older people had different values. Could they be horrified because she and Jed lived so close to each other? That hardly seemed creditable, but who knew?

Edith gave her a look straight out of the deep freezer. "You *look* ordinary," she announced in ringing tones that equated the word with an infestation of head lice. Turning, she swept through the door. Or would have, if her sister hadn't been in the way. Again there was a short tussle as they once again tried to get through the opening at the same time, but then, they popped through, and the door closed behind them.

A full two minutes later, Caitlin managed to crank her jaw up where it belonged and shut her mouth. "Ordinary?" she said. "Ordinary?"

That was bad?

She thought about the outfits they wore and glanced down at her own unadorned suit. Well, maybe it was to them. What business was it of theirs, anyway? It wasn't as if she and Jed were involved. Engaged. Married.

Insulted, Caitlin turned to the stairs and stomped up to her apartment. This was war, she decided. Poor Jed, putting up with those two busybodies all these years. He deserved a break from them.

And as for herself, Caitlin thought, she might be a lot of things, but she wasn't *ordinary!*

"I DON'T REALLY THINK they see my nephew in romantic terms," Geneva Bishop said. "At least I hope not."

Caitlin wasn't so sure. Geneva had called her as she usually did as soon as Caitlin opened her door on Tuesday morning. As she sipped her coffee and looked at the *Wall*

Street Journal, she'd told Geneva about the upcoming bachelor auction and the visit from the Carlton twins.

"Then what is it?" she asked.

"I think they feel proprietary toward him. Since I'm not there, they think they need to watch out for him."

"He's thirty years old and he's got oodles of family around here who could watch out for him," Caitlin said.

"Yes, but you see, they're incurably nosy and they think Jed should live an exciting life. They think everyone should, but for some reason, they've fixated on him. They think he's going to settle into being boring."

Or settle for someone ordinary, Caitlin thought, still miffed. "Jed could never be boring," she said.

"They're crazy," Geneva said flatly. "This could get tricky at the bachelor auction."

"No kidding."

"I'll have to give this some thought. Maybe I can come up with a suggestion to help you out. In the meantime, we have financial matters to discuss." She launched into a series of questions and comments that had Caitlin scrambling for answers.

Fifteen minutes later, Caitlin hung up, forgot about the Carlton twins and spent the rest of the day happily engaged in writing up various investment plans to propose to another of Geneva's friends. When Eunice arrived, they prepared a mailing for potential clients from a list Caitlin had acquired from the Chamber of Commerce. By the time five o'clock arrived, Caitlin was pleasantly tired and satisfied with the day's work. She had received a call from Jed's mother, who wanted her to speak to the women's club about investments. Caitlin had accepted eagerly and anticipated an increase in her clientele afterward.

Before leaving for the day, Caitlin gathered up her purse, briefcase and jacket and laid them on her desk, then went into the small washroom at the back of her office. When she came out, she was startled to see Reenie Starr sitting in the chair opposite her desk.

"Mrs. Starr!" Caitlin exclaimed, hurrying forward. "Hello."

Reenie looked up with a vague smile. "Hello, my dear. Isn't it a lovely day?"

Caitlin looked outside. Clouds were filling up the horizon. Rain had been forecast. "Um, yes," she said.

Seeing Caitlin's puzzled look, Reenie turned and glanced out the window. "Well, when did that happen?" she asked, shaking her head. She rapped her knuckles against her forehead. "You must think I've got a few cracked eggs."

Caitlin smiled. "Oh, no, Mrs. Starr."

Reenie's face pinched. "Oh, yes, you do, but you're wrong. I simply forget things sometimes. Just like you're forgetting to call me Reenie."

Caitlin settled herself on the corner of her desk. "We all do. In fact, I was so surprised to see you I forgot to tell you about my good fortune."

"Your car," Reenie said. "I heard about that. So the penny brought you luck?"

Caitlin opened her mouth to remind Reenie that the "penny" had actually been a flattened bottle cap and she wasn't so sure that was what had brought her the car, but she'd already hurt Reenie's feelings, so she said, "Yes, ma'am, and thank you."

Reenie's eyes narrowed shrewdly. "You don't sound like you mean that."

Caitlin answered with a weak shrug.

"I thought not," Reenie said with a sniff. She reached into the pocket of her black raincoat and pulled out something that dangled from a key chain. She handed this to Caitlin.

Caitlin stared at the basinlike object with the wooden water tank for several seconds before it made sense to her. "An old-fashioned toilet?" she asked.

Reenie's face turned pink with pleasure. "Actually we used to call them water closets. My late husband was a plumber, you know."

"No, I didn't know that," Caitlin said in a faint voice. "How...nice."

"I tried to find a rabbit's foot key chain for you, because it's a time-honored symbol of good luck—though probably not to the poor rabbit who used to own it," she added sadly. "But I couldn't find one, so I got you that, instead. It will bring you good luck and teach you another good lesson. As the penny did."

Caitlin wasn't quite sure why she was being the recipient of all these lessons in good fortune. She really couldn't think of what lesson she'd learned last Friday night, unless it was one on how to win a car, nearly get arrested for drunk driving, participate in breaking and entering, agree to buy Jed in a bachelor auction and almost end up making love to him all in one evening.

In other words, the Jed-Bishop-could-talk-her-into-anything lesson.

She eyed the key chain warily. She wasn't sure she was ready for another evening like that one.

Reenie stood suddenly. "It's time for me to go," she announced.

Caitlin scooted off her desk. "I was about to leave myself. Please let me drive you."

"No thank you, dear," Reenie said breezily. "I can manage."

"But it's going to rain."

Reenie turned and gave her a stern look. "I can manage," she repeated firmly. "Rain won't hurt me."

Caitlin subsided reluctantly. Managing on her own seemed to be very important to her new friend. "Well, okay."

With a satisfied nod, Reenie left the office. Caitlin took another look at her newest good-luck charm, laughed softly and quickly stuffed it into her purse. She turned off the lights and locked the door. Outside, she made a quick scan of the sidewalk. Reenie had disappeared.

"For a little old lady, she sure can hustle," Caitlin murmured. "Maybe she is some kind of spirit."

Thunder rumbled and rain began to spatter the ground. Caitlin cast another concerned look along the street, then climbed into her car and headed home.

THE STORM PICKED UP WATER and wind as it met the flow of air moving in from the Pacific, buffeting the old house. Caitlin was awakened from a fitful sleep by banging noises. Thinking it was another loose shutter, she turned over and put the pillow over her head when she heard her name called.

"Caitlin! Wake up. I'm drowning," Jed shouted from the hallway.

Startled into wakefulness, she bounded out of bed and stumbled from her room, fleeing toward his voice without thinking to turn on the light. She had heard him arrive home a little while before she'd gone to bed, but he hadn't been over to see her. Even though she wanted to tell him about the visit from Edith and Evelyn, she knew he was tired. She had told herself she wasn't disappointed she hadn't seen him.

"I'm coming," she yelled. "Hold on." She banged her knee into the edge of a table. "Oomph," she grunted as she careened against the corner of the sofa and tripped over the rug, finally half-falling against the door with a thud. "Ouch," she yelped as pain shot from her shoulder and knee.

"Cait, what's wrong? Are you okay?" he called through the door.

Fully awake now, she hit the switch for the overhead light. Wincing at its brightness, she tried to rub her knee and shoulder as she worked the locks on the door.

"Caitlin, answer me!"

"No, I'm not okay." She flung open the door and blinked at him. "What do you want?"

He stood barefoot in the drafty hallway wearing a white T-shirt with a stretched-out neck and baggy gray sweatpants. His black hair fell over his forehead in a tumble. A blanket and pillow were clutched to his chest. "I need a place to sleep," he said, giving her a forlorn look.

Caitlin frowned at him. "Try your bed," she suggested, and started to close the door on him.

Jed's hand shot out to keep it open. "I can't. It's wet."

"You wet the bed?"

He muffled a laugh. "*I* didn't, smart mouth. I forgot and left the window open while I was gone. The rain came in and soaked it. I'd sleep on the couch, but it's too short for me."

"Bend your knees," she suggested, and again tried to close the door. Jed was too quick for her. He simply pushed the door wide open, gathered her close and frog-stepped her backward into the apartment.

"Come on, Caitlin, have a heart. I've driven all the way from San Diego today. I gotta get some sleep." In the middle of this tale of woe, his gaze focused and roamed over her. "By the way, I like the spiked-hair look. It's sexy. Cute pj's, too. Did they come with bunny feet in them?"

Immediately shivers swept over her. To her alarm, her nipples peaked and pushed against the soft waffle-knit cotton of her pajamas. They *were* cute pajamas, and her favorites, long-sleeved and covered with tiny yellow rosebuds. To cover her reaction, she hunched her shoulders and crossed her arms at her waist. She gave him a disgruntled look. "My sofa is even shorter than yours," she said.

"Yeah, but it folds out into a bed."

"A very short one."

"And you've got that big ottoman I can put at the end for my feet." He was already hotfooting it toward the sofa and gathering up the pillows and cushions. "It'll be perfect."

"Well, 'perfect' is probably overstating it," she said grumpily, but she didn't insist that he leave. "I should throw you out."

He glanced up with a grin, looking rumpled and sexy himself with his sweatpants riding low on his hips and his clean white T-shirt a contrast to his tanned skin. His smile was pleased and more than a little smug. "The fact that you aren't proves that your good judgment is—"

"On vacation." Her toes curled against the cold floor and she shivered again. "Someplace warm, no doubt."

"Still working strong, even when you're awakened at midnight," he finished, ignoring her interruption.

"Humph," she said, but in the bright light of the apartment she could see that his face was lined with exhaustion. He did need sleep and she was being petty to deny him a place on her couch. Really, the only reason she was reluctant was that the sight of him had her thinking lustful thoughts, which were making her weak in the knees.

Mentally she gave herself a thump on the back of the head. *Be strong, girl,* she thought. *You can take it.*

Turning, she strode briskly to the linen closet in her bedroom and returned with some sheets and another blanket. As he made his bed and scooted the ottoman to the end, she stood back and watched. He was really very efficient. She recalled how impressed she'd been with the cleanliness of his apartment the night they'd slept— *Never mind.*

"What's been going on around here while I've been gone?" he asked as he tucked in the sheet.

Caitlin told him about the work Terry and Barney had been doing and about the strange encounter with the Carlton twins—though she left out their statement that she was ordinary. That still stung.

He winced. "Maybe I shouldn't have asked you to help me out. This bachelor auction could get ugly."

"I grew up in a tough neighborhood," she said absently. "I can handle it."

He tossed the pillow onto the bed and turned to her. "A tough neighborhood?"

Before he could ask her any more about that, she said, "Besides, I've got a new good-luck charm. Mrs. Starr came by today and gave me a toilet."

"*What?*"

Caitlin told him about the encounter with Reenie. She took the water-closet key chain from her purse and showed it to him.

He took it from her and examined it, then handed it back. "She thinks this will bring you luck? Hey, what's wrong?"

Caitlin was rubbing her knee and shoulder, which were still smarting.

"I banged into the table and the door while trying to

rescue you from drowning," she said in a disgruntled tone.

"You deserve a medal. You were wounded while trying to save a comrade." Dropping the blanket, he moved closer to examine her injuries.

Caitlin tried to bat him away, but he simply picked her up and deposited her on his newly made bed, then tugged up the leg of her pajamas to inspect the red spot on her knee. "Well, see, here's your problem right here."

"What?" She tried to struggle upright, but he held her down with a hand on her uninjured shoulder.

"Your knee's too bony. See, it sticks out right here, begging for things to bang into it."

"It is *not* bony." She tried again to sit up, but he held her back, gently but firmly.

"Quit wiggling. I've got to see if it's okay."

"Bishop, it's not a major trauma. I only bumped it."

"You never know," he responded in a somber tone. He picked up a brass candlestick that sat on the end table, wrapped it in the corner of the blanket and tapped the reflex area below her kneecap. Her foot flew into the air.

"Seems okay," he approved.

"I wish it had kicked you," she said, sitting up stiffly. She eyed the candlestick as he set it back on the table. "Where'd you learn to do that, anyway?"

"I used to date an orthopedic surgeon," he said. "An expert on anatomy. She taught me everything I know."

"I'll bet."

"Now let me look at your shoulder." He tugged at the neck of her pajama top, his clever fingers making quick work of unbuttoning the buttons.

"Stop!" she yelped, grabbing for the front of her top. "My shoulder is fine."

His eyebrows drew together. "Can't be too sure. It might be dislocated."

"I'd be in agony if it was. Didn't your orthopedic girlfriend teach you that?"

"Honey," he growled, "you'd be amazed what I learned from that woman."

"No, I wouldn't," she responded sweetly.

He answered her with a leering grin as he eased her pajama top off her shoulder and gave her creamy skin an appreciative once-over. "Looks okay to me," he said. His head lowered and his lips brushed her skin. "In fact, it looks great." He kissed her shoulder blade. "Couldn't be better."

Heat sizzled through her. Her voice was thin and reedy as she said, "Uh, Jed?"

"Yeah?" His breath whispered against her skin.

"It's, uh…the other shoulder."

He paused and looked up. "I knew that. I *did*," he said defensively as her eyes widened in disbelief. "I thought this one might be hurting in sympathy. And don't look at me like my cheese is slipping off its cracker."

The desire building in her eased a bit and she giggled. He responded with a comical wiggle of his eyebrows.

Against her better judgment, Caitlin relaxed. Enthralled as usual by his method of getting what he wanted, she stopped fighting him. How could Edith and Evelyn ever think he might settle for a boring life?

Turning her head, she looked into his face, inches from her own. His eyes were teasing and testing her, his hands warm and vital on her skin as he pulled up one side of her pajama top and smoothed the other off her throbbing shoulder.

With his gaze holding hers, Jed massaged her skin, his fingers rubbing over the flesh and then working deep to ease the tension that had tightened her muscles at the moment of his touch. He placed a kiss at the base of her neck. "Why are you so tense, honey?"

"Because you're kissing me."

He laughed. "You know, some people think that's a good thing." He opened his mouth against her skin and the heat of his breath seared her.

"Oooh, it's a good thing all right," she answered. Heat, awareness, fright and wonder all bounded through her, chasing away the need to resist him. Words came to her mind, but couldn't make the journey to her lips.

Delight and dread warred in her as Jed lowered his head once again and caressed her skin softly with his lips. When she moved restively, he murmured, "It's all right, Caitlin."

She didn't know if he meant her shoulder or her needs, which he seemed to understand.

"I'm sorry you hurt yourself on account of me," he said. "I won't let it happen again."

Caitlin couldn't look away from the solemn promise in his gray eyes. What was he promising? Was he giving her some kind of talisman against physical pain? Mental? Emotional? A vow that, whatever happened, he would keep her from being hurt? That couldn't be it, her practical nature insisted. No one could make that kind of promise to another person.

But maybe. Her needs and desires yearned to believe such a promise. If so, she should grab on to it, hold that promise, because she would certainly need it later. "Jed, I—"

"Don't say anything," he instructed, lifting his lips from her shoulder. Drawing her along with him, he lay back on the bed so that she lay sprawled across his chest. She had forgotten that her top was unbuttoned, but the brush of his soft T-shirt against her breasts reminded her. In a moment of panicked confusion, she put her hands on his shoulders and arched upward. Her breasts lifted from his chest, her nipples peaked and hardened. Stunned, she watched as his gaze went from her face to her breasts, then back to meet her eyes, which were staring at him.

"Well, now," he said in a low, rumbling voice. "That's about the prettiest sight I ever saw."

Caitlin whimpered.

"What's the matter, Cait?"

She swallowed. "I...I think that if sanity's going to put in an appearance, now might be a good time."

He lifted his head and she could see that his eyes were deep and mysterious. "Haven't you heard, Cait? Sanity's way overrated."

Her lips trembled. "I...I don't know about that...."

"Shut up and kiss me, Cait."

She started to answer, to say, "Okay," but she only got as far as forming the *O,* which seemed to suit Jed fine, because he fit his lips onto hers and kissed her with deep thoroughness as if he wanted her to remember this kiss, to compare it to every other one. There was no comparison, though. The touch of his lips, teeth and tongue had wildly erotic thoughts blossoming in her mind.

Her hands came up and around his shoulders. She kissed him back, delighting in the taste and texture of him, his tenderness and warmth. At that moment she couldn't remember why she'd run from him that time, weeks ago, when he'd given her such pleasure, made her feel so treasured and wanted. Hazy thoughts of not wanting to be temporary in his life or to be one of the many women who dangled after him, of him saying he wasn't the marrying kind, drifted through her, but didn't stay. She didn't want to think about those things. She wanted to feel him, his solid weight on her, his strength filling her. She wanted...so many things she couldn't put into words, but she would try.

"This is really, really nice," she murmured, her lips against his jaw. It was a truly wonderful jaw—strong, definite, smooth. *Smooth?* She drew away and gave him a dubious look. "Did you shave before you came over here?"

He'd been giving the base of her throat his undivided attention, but now he lifted his head. "Yeah. Why?"

"Were you hoping that we would...?" She gestured to the sofa bed beneath them.

"And if I was?"

"Don't answer a question with a question," she instructed, but then his hand moved from her waist to her breast. "Doh...ho...nn't distract me."

"Then answer my question first."

"I...think you...must be...a real optimist," she moaned.

He chuckled softly and moved his hand in a slow rotation. It sent her heart into a pounding rhythm that would have made any flamenco dancer proud. "Oh, yeah?" he mocked. "But so you know, I shaved because I forgot my razor when I left for San Diego and I was pretty grubby after two days in Steve's rig."

"Ohhh," she breathed, drawing out the word on a thread of desire. She was almost sure she'd had some clever thing ready to say, but it had vaporized along with her common sense. "I'm glad," she confessed, instead. "It feels so good. You smell so good."

"Oh, honey." Jed buried his nose against her throat. "If this is a feel-good-smell-good contest, you win."

"Thank you." Leaning away, she blinked at him, her

tawny eyes gone smoky with desire. "Why don't you kiss me again and let's see how that feels?"

The slumberous desire in her eyes combined with the moist fullness of her lips and her flushed face, telling Jed that he could make love to her now to their mutual delight. She would be with him every step of the way.

Jed did as she'd asked, kissing her with the passion that was rising inside him like an irresistible tide. But a tiny voice of conscience insisted on being heard. What would happen in the morning? Would she run from him again? This might turn out to be another of his plans that went awry.

And it had all started because he'd missed her. Damn, how he'd missed her the past two days. He'd thought a dozen times about calling her, but what would he have said? That he couldn't go another mile without hearing her voice?

How could he do that and maintain his image as an easygoing, laid-back guy who never let serious thoughts about a woman interfere with his life? He couldn't, that was all. He liked helping people, doing things for them, but he didn't like to get too deeply involved in their lives. And even if he *had* been thinking in terms of commitment, he knew *she* wasn't.

The very act of *thinking* the word "wife" made his mouth go dry. Neither of them were ready for that, in spite of the attraction that simmered and occasionally boiled between them.

Slowly, carefully, he rebuttoned her top. "You'll be fine. Nothing's hurt beyond repair."

She blinked, still fighting her way out of the sensual haze he'd created. "Hurt?"

"Your shoulder."

"What about it?"

His lips twitched. "You bumped it. I was checking it. Remember?"

"Oh." She pulled air into her lungs, but the increase in oxygen didn't seem to help the function of her brain. "Sure. Sure I do," she lied.

Jed shook his head, seemed to be trying to swallow a laugh and sat up, pulling her with him. He managed to get them both to their feet.

"Thanks for the bed," he said, standing suddenly and lifting her to her feet. "We both need to get some sleep."

Dazed, she turned toward her room. "Yes, I, um… That's a good idea." She wanted to say something more, to leave him with a quick retort or rebuttal, but none came to her mind. She looked at him, her eyes full of questions and uncertainties, then turned and went into her bedroom. She closed the door carefully behind her and leaned against it.

Why had he stopped? Because neither of them was ready. That much was obvious, even to her mushy brain. She felt buffeted by unfulfilled desire, but she should be grateful to him for stopping. One of them had to show some sense. They had made love once before and it had complicated things. Neither of them needed that to happen again.

It was good that he had stopped, she thought. Good. She nodded decisively and headed for her bed, then took a right turn and marched to the bathroom for a cold shower.

7

"Now remember, Cait, I'm depending on you." Jed knotted his tie, straightened the ends, made a sound of disgust and ripped out the knot. Why couldn't he get the damned thing right?

"I know." Caitlin was standing by his bed, leaning up against the tall corner post of the footboard. She was watching him with undisguised amusement.

"No matter how much money Miss Edith and Miss Evelyn bid, you've got to bid more."

"I understand, Jed."

He turned from the mirror and gave her a suspicious look. "Have you ever been to an auction before? Any kind of auction?"

He didn't like the innocent shrug she gave him. "No."

"Things could get nasty," he muttered. "Real nasty."

She lifted an eyebrow at him. "Jed, it's not like we're going into combat."

"That's what you think. You've met the Carlton twins. Do they look like the type to give up easily?"

"Well, no."

"They've been calling my family members all week, including my sister-in-law, Mary, who doesn't need the extra stress since she's about to go into labor any minute, and my aunt Geneva in L.A., who told them to mind their own business."

"What have they been calling about?"

Jed turned back to the mirror. Hell, he should have kept his mouth shut. After their near lovemaking episode, they had gone back to their usual prickly, bantering relationship. It was best that way, he was sure of it, and she seemed to agree, because she hadn't mentioned it, either.

He whipped the end of the tie around and made a new knot. "I wish I didn't have to wear this damned thing," he groused.

"You've retied it four times," Caitlin said. Walking up behind him, she put her hand on his shoulder and urged him around. Batting his hands away, she adjusted the knot herself. Jed liked the feel of her hands brushing the underside of his jaw. He liked the scent of her perfume as it subtly teased his sense of smell. He heartily approved of the new dress she was wearing. It wasn't one of her usual business suits, which he detested. And it wasn't as sexy as the blue dress she'd worn the night she'd won the car. This one was pale lavender, almost the color of smoke with a short, snug skirt that did great things for her already perfect legs. The top was a little too modest and high-necked, but hey, he wasn't complaining. At least it didn't have the battalion of buttons that usually graced her clothing. This one had an easily accessible zipper that—

"What were the Carlton twins calling your family about?" she asked again.

He gave a start when she cut into his fantasy, and he realized how far he'd let his mind wander. A quick look at her intently interested face told him he'd be wise to stick to his original topic of conversation.

"I've always hated ties ever since my days at Sunday school when I had to wear one to please my mother. Now, here I am at thirty, and still doing things to please her."

"Jed?"

"Did you have to wear uncomfortable clothes to Sunday school to please your mother?" he asked.

"My mother wasn't the churchgoing type, Jed. Answer my question. What have the Carlton twins been calling your family about?"

"Uh, nothing, I— Aargh!" he squawked as she tightened the knot on his tie and cut off the circulation to his brain. "Ca-ait," he wheezed, reaching for her wrists. "Stop."

She loosened the knot, but he didn't like the determined look in her eyes.

"All right, all right. They've been trying to get information about you. About whether or not your intentions toward me are honorable."

"Are you kidding?"

"Now, Cait, that shouldn't surprise you, considering their visit here on Monday," he soothed. "They're protective of me."

"They're nuts," she muttered.

"True, and that's why you need to watch yourself during the bidding. You've got the money?"

"Every penny you wiped out of your bank account." She paused and chewed her lip, an unconscious action he found wildly erotic. He wondered if she'd let him have a go at it. Probably not, he decided with a sigh. After the kiss they'd shared a few nights ago, she'd gone back to treating him with her usual breeziness, but she might as well have a big sign attached to her chest saying, "Touch me and die." If he tried to take a taste of her lips, she'd probably bite his tongue. But damn, it might be worth a try in spite of his determination not to get serious about her.

Before he could do anything idiotic, she stepped back,

gave him a worried look and said, "If I pay a lot of money for you, people won't get the wrong idea, will they?"

"That depends."

"On what?"

"On how much money you think is a *lot* of money."

She tilted her head and considered him. "For you, anything more than fifty-seven cents."

"If that's as high as you're willing to go, you're dooming me to another evening of broken dentures and elbows in the ribs." He wiggled his eyebrows at her. "But the higher you're willing to go, the more attractive I'll seem."

"Well, that's a terrible burden to have to bear, but that's not what I was thinking. I was wondering if people will think that I, a financial adviser, was being foolish with my money."

His expression collapsed into a frown. "Here we go again. Why do you worry so much about what people think? The *Clarion* came out day before yesterday and you haven't had huge numbers of clients calling up to cancel their dealings with you, now have you?"

"Jed, I don't *have* huge numbers of clients in the first place."

"But how many calls have you received since Wednesday congratulating you on your car and asking about your financial services?"

Caitlin looked down at her hands. "A few."

"A few?"

She tossed her head back and stuck her chin out at him. "Oh, all right, many. I've had many calls. You were right and I was wrong and I shouldn't have been so worried about the photo, even though I looked like a deer caught in headlights."

"So why are you *still* worried about what people will

think? I've never known anybody who worries about that as much as you do."

"Says the man who wants me to pay a lot of money for him so people will think he's attractive." She rolled her eyes. "Jed, people *know* you're attractive. All they have to do is look at you, and besides, all those women you've got parading through this place are testimony to that." She turned away. "Hadn't we better go?"

He wasn't going to let her get away with that, either. He reached out and snagged her hand. "I want you to pay a lot for me so Edith and Evelyn won't, but, honey, I didn't realize it bothered you that so many of my friends are women."

"Good heavens, why should it bother me?" she asked evasively.

"That's what I'm wondering. I also didn't realize you think I'm attractive."

She lifted her free hand and examined her fingernails. "Oh?"

He kept a firm grip on her hand. He wanted answers. "Are we talking people-don't-run-screaming-when-they-see-me attractive or baby-I'm-hot-for-your-body attractive?"

Her eyes grew wary. "Not-ashamed-to-be-seen-with-you-in-public attractive." She wrenched her hand from his and glanced at her watch. "My goodness, look at the time. We'd better go."

She whirled away, snatched up the handbag she'd laid on his bed when he'd called her into his apartment to help him with his tie, then seemed to realize exactly where she was and skittered away from the bed. He lifted his hand to hide a grin as she hotfooted it out of the bedroom and marched across his living room. He was making her nervous, or being in his apartment was making her nervous. For some crazy reason he didn't mind that at all.

He grabbed his wallet and keys, snagged his navy blue blazer off its hanger and followed her out the door. He'd been dreading this night for weeks, but now he was beginning to think it might get pretty interesting.

"SOLD TO THE LADY in the red dress for eight hundred dollars, a date with one bachelor by the name of Ted Wilkinson and the romantic day he's planned on his sailboat." The auctioneer, who happened to be Jed's uncle Frank, looked up and grinned as Ted left the small stage that had been set up at the front of the room. "I've sailed with Ted, young lady," he said. "I suggest you pack some motion-sickness pills."

The crowd laughed and settled down to wait for the next bachelor to appear. Caitlin looked around the large main room of the women's club, which was packed with club members, bidders and people from the community who had dropped in to enjoy the fun. And it was fun. Her idea of a women's club had been blue-haired ladies sitting around drinking tea and gossiping. This one seemed to have its share of older women, but there were lots of younger ones, too, and they all appeared to have embraced the single goal of making this auction a success. Mrs. Bishop had greeted her with warm enthusiasm and reminded her of her promise to be a speaker at one of their upcoming meetings. Seeing the diversity of the group, Caitlin was already planning a talk that would cover everything from college finances to individual retirement accounts. She should join the group herself. After all, she was a member of the community now.

Warily she eyed the Carlton twins, who sat two rows in front of her and had turned around several times already to throw dark looks in her direction. Did they know she was going to bid on Jed? Or were they still perturbed that such an ordinary woman as she was had the nerve to attend the auction? Whatever. The next few minutes were going to be dicey.

The two ladies were dressed to kill in sequined spandex dresses—lime green tonight. They also wore feathered boas of the same color and purple hats decorated with ostrich plumes. The people behind them had to duck and dart around in order to see.

Frank interrupted her thoughts. "Our next eligible bachelor is my nephew Jed Bishop." When his name was called, Jed stepped from a curtained area beside the stage and mounted the steps.

He was almost knocked over by the sigh of pleasure that went around the room. Caitlin couldn't have agreed more. He looked fabulous. His midnight hair was perfectly combed, his jaw was freshly shaven and the navy blue blazer he wore complemented his eyes and hugged the substantial width of his shoulders. He glanced up and grinned, then aimed a wink in her direction. At least she thought it was in her direction, but most of the other women must have thought so, too, because there was a collective intake of breath as if he'd stopped half the hearts in the room.

Caitlin put her hand over her own pounding heart. If this kept up, the women's club would be handing out pacemakers before the evening was over.

"The date Jed is offering will be an evening of dinner and theater in San Francisco," Frank went on. "Finishing up with a romantic midnight cruise around the bay. Let's start the bidding at one hundred dollars."

Before Caitlin could even open her mouth, six women were on their feet, shouting. She had only a moment to recognize Maria Rossi and Raeann Forbes before Edith and Evelyn Carlton joined the melee, shooting upward and hollering out their bids in voices that could have summoned hogs from a faraway bog.

Frank stumbled back, and Jed, looking stunned himself, had to grab him and hold him upright. It took Frank a few seconds to collect himself, but he finally got the bidders under control, though he couldn't seem to keep the amounts from leaping upward a hundred dollars at a time. Caitlin joined in the bidding, but fearing she couldn't be heard, stood up like the other bidders and called out her offer.

One by one, the other women dropped out, giving disappointed shrugs or laughing with their friends. Pretty soon, it was down to only Caitlin bidding against the Carlton twins, who turned and gave her drop-dead looks whenever she called out a bid. They seemed to think they were the only ones who should bid on Jed because that was the way it had always been. Caitlin would have felt sorry for them if they hadn't been so nasty about ordinariness. She smoothed the short skirt of the dress she'd bought for the occasion. Ordinary, indeed!

"The bid stands at two thousand dollars," Frank called. He glanced over at his sister-in-law. Jed's mother shook her head as if she couldn't believe it, either. "Do I hear two thousand one hundred?"

"You bet you do," shrieked Edith.

"Two thousand three hundred," Caitlin called.

The Carltons turned and gave her looks that promised dire revenge. Caitlin answered with a confident smile. She was actually beginning to enjoy this, but there was still a part of her that didn't want them to be angry at her.

The Carlton twins faced the front, squared their shoulders, and Evelyn called out, "Three thousand."

A collective gasp traveled around the room. This was far more than any of the other bachelors had brought in. Caitlin gulped. Jed had given her three thousand to bid on him, saying it would never go that high. The last time he'd been involved in this, Edith and Evelyn had paid only half that amount for a date with him.

Caitlin's eyes shot to Jed's face, which was turning pale. He sent her a panicked look. She started to shrug, indicating she didn't know what to do, but out of the corner of her eye, she saw Edith turn and give her a smug, superior smile, indicating she was sure they'd won.

Oh, yeah? Mentally Caitlin pushed up her sleeves, spit on her hands and got ready to fight. The heck with caring if they got angry at her. They were the ones who had turned this into a personal campaign by calling her ordinary, then asking Jed's family about her. Stretching onto her toes, she called out, "Three thousand five hundred."

Jed jerked as if someone had zapped him with a cattle prod. His gaze swung to her face. She gave him a firm nod and he grinned. He knew she was into her own money now.

The people around them were beginning to realize that there was something personal going on here. All eyes fixed on Edith and Evelyn to see what they'd do next. They held a hurried consultation and Edith called out, "Four thousand."

Like fans at a tennis match, everyone in the room turned to Caitlin, who blanched momentarily, but then decided to fight on. Jed was depending on her! He'd been telling her that for a week. She couldn't let him down. Looking up, she saw that he was watching her with admiration for the determination she was showing. That was all very fine, she thought, nearly hyperventilating when Edith and Evelyn glared at her again, but he wasn't the one the Carlton twins were plotting to sell into white slavery! She broke out in a sweat and someone nearby handed her a tissue. With a hurried thanks, she blotted her forehead, wadded the tissue and called out, "Five thousand."

Attention whipped back to the Carltons. Evelyn was the spokesperson this time. She gave Caitlin a "top this" look and called out, "Six thousand."

Tossing her head, excited and high on adrenaline, Caitlin kicked off her shoes, climbed onto her chair, threw her hands into the air and yelled. "Seven thousand dollars!" Looking directly at the two ladies, she tacked on, "Ha!"

The Carltons threw her a look that should have killed her on the spot and sat down abruptly. Clutching their purses in their laps, they stared straight ahead.

"Sold to the lady on the chair," Frank called. The room erupted into cheers, Caitlin looked down, dazed to realize that she was, indeed, standing on her chair. Embarrassment swept through her, but before she could clamber down, Jed bolted off the stage, rushed to her and whipped his arms around her waist. Laughing, he swept her down into his arms and kissed her. The room went wild with whistles and catcalls.

Caitlin threw her arms around his neck and kissed him back, then drew away and said in shock, "I bid seven thousand dollars for a date," she gasped. "With you!"

He laughed and kissed her again. "Don't sound so horrified. Maybe you'll get your money's worth."

"I'd better," she answered as he set her back on her feet and steadied her while she tried to find her shoes and the audience laughed and clapped. She glanced around, accepting congratulations and thinking that the crazy things that had happened to her and that she'd done in the past week had made her feel like more a part of the community than she ever had before. When Jed's arm clamped around her waist and he drew her to him, she realized that home wasn't simply a place, it was a feeling and she felt it in this room, with this man.

Shaken by the knowledge, she pushed away from him, gave him a trembling smile and sat down. The people seated nearby rearranged themselves so that Jed could have the seat next to her. He parked himself there and accepted the congratulations of the crowd. Looking quite pleased with himself, he stretched his arm across the back of Caitlin's chair and sat back, ready to enjoy the rest of the auction.

Caitlin gave him a sidelong look. "Don't let this go to your head," she advised.

"Too late, honey," he said, flashing his devilish grin at her. "There's something about having women fighting over me that really gives my ego a boost."

She smiled sweetly. "If your ego had any more of a boost, it could fling the space shuttle into orbit."

He grinned and turned away as his uncle began the bidding on the next bachelor. The frenzy of bidding on Jed had started the ball rolling, and the next several men carried high price tags. By the time it was over, the book fund had nearly fifteen thousand dollars in it and Jed's mother appeared to be on the verge of fainting.

Jed glanced over his shoulder as they walked to her car and said, "Uh-oh."

"What is it?" she asked, busily digging in her purse for her keys. She felt an incredible light-headedness that she knew was a result of the adrenaline rush she'd just been through. She hoped it wouldn't affect her driving. She glanced around to see that Edith and Evelyn were bearing down on them. "Uh-oh is right," she said.

"Jed, it looks as though this is the end of our friendship," Miss Edith announced.

Jed cast a quick glance at Caitlin. "It is, Miss Edith? Well, I'm sorry to hear that, but why can't we still be friends?"

"Because you and this girl have embarrassed us," Evelyn answered primly. "This was a setup between the two of you, wasn't it?"

"Yes, it was."

Caitlin gave him a swift glance. She hadn't expected him to lie, but she hadn't thought he'd be so quick to admit the truth, either, to these two nosy ladies.

"Humph," Evelyn said. "All these years we've been looking out for you, trying to keep you from having a dull life and now we see it meant nothing to you. We thought we were your friends, but you've embarrassed us in front of the whole town."

Jed nodded his head. "I understand how you feel, but the truth is, I finally realized I'm not good enough for the two of you."

Caitlin's eyes widened and she choked back a laugh.

Edith glared at Jed. "What do you mean?"

He dropped his head as if he was ashamed of himself, then lifted it to stare earnestly at them. "The date we had for the last bachelor auction wasn't very good. It was my fault. I know that, but you two were so kind and bravely carried on trying to make it seem like you were having a good time with me." His frown deepened. "But I know the truth. I bored you, didn't I?"

The Carltons looked taken aback. "Why, we didn't—"

"Oh, don't try to deny it," Jed said, lifting his hand and assuming the air of a martyr. "Sure, I'm young, but I'm boring. I know it and I accept it. The two of you are too kind to say it, but it's true. I know you felt obligated to continue trying to change me, but I think we all know it's hopeless. I'm in a rut and the worst part is, I like being in a rut."

Caitlin stared, amazed at the web of fabrications he was weaving. She wondered if he would catch himself in it. She glanced at the Carlton twins. They exchanged looks.

"I didn't mean to embarrass you tonight and neither did Caitlin," Jed went on, "but I felt like it was better to make a clean break and not saddle you with someone as boring as me." The look he gave them was as soulful as an injured puppy's.

Edith lifted her hand. "But this girl—"

"She's boring, too," Jed said morosely. "That's good in an investment counselor, though, in case you ever need her help or advice."

Talk about damned with faint praise. Under her breath, Caitlin muttered, "Don't do me any favors, Bishop."

He was still talking. "In fact, we're going to go home now. She'll go into her apartment and read the *Wall Street Journal* and then go to bed and drink a glass of warm milk. I'll go to my apartment and watch television. My favorite science program is on—'All About Fungus.'"

Evelyn looked stunned and then sympathy began to show in her eyes. "But your date in San Francisco? That'll be exciting." She glanced at her sister. "At least we thought so."

"Yeah, maybe, but I like things to be calm, you know. The play we're going to see is very avant-garde. The actors sit on stage and don't move for two hours."

"They don't move?"

"Not a muscle, and the cruise around the bay is actually a medical test for a new motion-sickness pill. If I don't barf, they'll pay me fifty dollars."

Caitlin erupted into violent coughs as she choked back a whoop of laughter and fought the tears of mirth in her eyes. Frantically she scrambled in her purse for a tissue, found one wrapped around something hard and angular. It took her a moment to realize it was the old-fashioned water-closet key chain Reenie had given her.

Jed lifted his hand. "See what I mean? Caitlin is a good friend. She did this so you wouldn't feel obligated to buy me at the auction, but she's in tears at the thought of having to go out with me. Aren't you, Cait?"

"Yes. Really, ladies, I wish you'd find someone else to help. He's hopeless."

Jed held out his hands to Edith and Evelyn, who grasped them and gave him looks of intense pity. "You've got to forget about me," he said. "You've got to let me live my boring life. I truly wish you'd find someone else. Someone more worthy of your interest. In fact, something's been worrying me." He manufactured a concerned look. "You don't think dullness is contagious, do you, Caitlin?"

Now what? She cleared her throat. "It's hard to say."

"Oh." As one, Edith and Evelyn dropped his hands and backed away.

"I...I see what you mean," Edith said. "You're... you're absolutely right. We need to use our energy, our enthusiasm for...for life, to help someone else." She grabbed her sister's arm and dragged her away. "Good night, Jed, and, uh, Caitlin. We'll see you."

The two women hurried across to their car and left with a squeal of tires.

"You're not good enough for them? You're boring? *I'm* boring? Where did you come up with that?"

He gave her a self-satisfied grin. "Pretty good, huh? I mean, considering it was spur-of-the-moment. I should have realized they'd be embarrassed and angry. I had to placate them somehow."

"Oh, I think they were placated. They also think you're crazy."

He opened the car door for her and then closed it after she'd slid behind the wheel. Climbing into the passenger side, he made himself comfortable and said, "Maybe they'll find a new interest in life, though, and stop crocheting booties for me."

"Have you considered introducing them to Terry Appletree and Barney Mellin? Now *there's* a couple of interesting men."

Jed grinned in agreement. As she started the car, she glanced down, surprised to see she still held the key chain. In fact, she'd been holding it when she'd said she wished the Carlton twins would find someone else to help. Maybe that wish would come true, she thought, dropping it into her purse, and there would be two fewer women making the pilgrimage to Jed's apartment. She would have less competition, and... Whoa!

"What's the matter?" Jed asked.

"Nothing." Her voice shot up, then dropped. "Nothing."

"You sound like you've got the hiccups."

"I'm fine." She pulled out of the parking lot and started home.

He didn't look like he believed her, but he changed the subject. "About the date we're going on..."

"To watch stationary actors in an avant-garde play, then take part in a motion-sickness study?"

"I really know how to show a woman a good time, don't I?"

"I can't wait."

"Good. When shall we go?"

She shot him a teasing glance. He was too full of himself right now, she decided. "How about a year from next Friday?"

"Next Friday? Sounds good," he answered breezily. "You gonna let me drive your car?"

"In your dreams."

They launched into an argument that carried them all the way home and up the stairs to their apartments. It broke off only when Jed heard his phone ringing and hurried inside to answer it. Caitlin went into her own apartment and closed the door, then wandered restlessly from the living room to the bedroom and back. After the excitement of the auction, their crazy conversation with Edith and Evelyn, then their argument on the way home, her *apartment* seemed boring. Being with Jed was fun. Far too much fun for her peace of mind, she decided ruefully. The thought of going out on an actual date with him set her stomach fluttering with excitement.

When she heard a knock on the door, she hurried over to find Jed standing there. His eyes were shining. "Mary's in labor," he announced. "Two weeks early."

"Oh. Do you think everything will be all right?"

"Yeah, Steve says so." Jed paced into her apartment and then turned. "That was him on the phone. He was on his way to drive a rig to Boise, but was called back because of Mary. I'm going to go in his place. I'll be gone a couple of days."

"Okay," Caitlin answered, hearing the way her voice dipped into the toes of her shoes.

"You'll have to keep tabs on Terry and Barney while I'm gone. They know you're my partner, so what you say goes."

"Yes, of course." Knowing they were on the same side gave Caitlin an inexplicable glow of happiness. "Maybe

I'll set them up with Edith and Evelyn while you're gone."

"Do that, and don't forget we have a date next Friday night," he said, pointing a finger at her. "And don't even *think* of trying to get out of it."

Eyes wide, she said, "I wouldn't dare."

He bent from the waist and gave her a peck on the cheek. "Good girl. You're learning."

"The truth is, I don't want to miss out on the opportunity to go out with someone as boring as you. Besides, what if Edith and Evelyn ask about our date? I'll need to tell them how many times I drifted off to sleep during the play."

"I don't think that will happen," he said, his eyes twinkling. "I forgot to mention that in the play the actors sitting perfectly still for two hours are also buck naked." With a laugh and a wink, he gave her another kiss and whisked out the door. "I'll call you," he said.

Smiling, Caitlin closed her door. This place was going to be awfully quiet for the next couple of days. In a few minutes she heard his footsteps going down the hall, and then the house was as silent as she'd predicted. Thinking of him on the road and of Mary in labor, Caitlin was too keyed up to sleep.

She couldn't believe she'd added thousands of dollars of her own money to buy a date with him at the auction. Even more surprising, she was glad she'd done it, which showed exactly how much she had changed in the past few weeks. She felt ashamed of the way she had snapped and skirmished with him over the house and so many other things, and even though she said teasingly that she didn't want to go out with him, she was looking forward to their date.

Caitlin moved around the room straightening a few

things, then paused when she heard the downstairs door. Had Jed forgotten something? Or had he forgotten to lock the door and it had been caught by the wind that was beginning to kick up?

She walked out into the hallway. "Jed?" When there was no answer, she descended the stairs. The door was standing open. With a shake of her head, she closed and locked it, then started back to her apartment. She happened to turn her head as she passed the parlor, then whirled around with a gasp of surprise when she saw who was there.

Reenie Starr sat on an old chair in front of the empty fireplace.

8

WITH A YELP, Caitlin fell back, her hand to her throat.

The old woman turned to look at her. "Hello, Caitlin dear. I'm sorry I startled you."

"Mrs. Starr, Reenie," Caitlin gasped, swallowing to force her heart down to its proper place. "Where did you come from?"

Reenie blinked at her. "Well, from home, of course, and then right through your front door. You were very thoughtful to leave it open for me."

"But what are you doing here?" Caitlin asked as she approached. "It's going to storm soon." As if in emphasis, thunder rumbled, moving ever closer.

"That's all right, dear. I'm dressed for it." She indicated the rain boots, yellow rain slicker and white rain hat she wore.

"You didn't walk here, did you?" Caitlin asked in alarm. "It's very dangerous to be out on the road at—"

"I'm fine," Reenie said, waving Caitlin's concern away. She held out the hem of the coat. "See? This has been decorated with some kind of reflective paint, exactly like a highway sign. Remarkable."

Caitlin smiled at the wonder in the old woman's voice. "Where did you get it?"

"Oh, I happened to walk by the fire station and there were several of these hanging right inside the door. Wasn't that considerate of the firefighters? The people in this town are so nice. I traded my black raincoat for it. It's very dangerous to be walking around at night in such dark clothes.'' She looked down at her new attire with pleasure. ''I'll have to return it, of course, as soon as I'm finished with it.'' Her voice was edged with regret. ''Too bad, but I suppose it *is* rather heavy for everyday wear.''

Caitlin bit her lip to keep from laughing. She could imagine the surprise of a member of the Crystal Cove volunteer fire department if he ran in to grab his equipment and ended up with a little old lady's sensible raincoat, instead. ''I think returning it would be a good idea,'' she said. ''It might be needed.''

''I suppose so,'' Reenie said sadly.

''Mrs. Starr, why are you out on a night like this? Didn't you know it's going to rain?''

''Oh, yes, but I had to come and talk to you. It's very important. Won't you sit down?'' She wriggled in her chair and sat back, then folded her hands in her lap and gave Caitlin an expectant look as if she was ready to tell a story.

''Of course,'' Caitlin said. ''But why don't we go up to my apartment? I've got the heat on and it's much more comfortable than this drafty room.''

Reenie pulled her coat around her. ''I'm perfectly comfortable here,'' she said. ''And besides, I can only stay a minute.'' Her voice took on an urgency that had Caitlin removing a stack of fireplace tiles and a tube of caulking from a rickety folding chair and pulling it up opposite the old woman.

''What is it, Mrs. Starr?''

''I don't think I'll ever get you to call me Reenie,'' the woman said. ''Well, never mind. I guess it's understandable, considering your line of work. Most of your clients are my age. Lots of people nowadays don't respect age, you know," she said in a regretful tone. "That's not why I'm here, though. I came to ask if the key chain helped you at the bachelor auction tonight."

"I'm not sure if it brought me luck or not." Caitlin explained what had happened at the auction and in the parking lot afterward.

"Well, then, I would say it did," Reenie answered, her eyes twinkling. "You have a date with Jed and he might be free of the attentions of Edith and Evelyn." She sniffed. "They were always silly girls."

"Oh, you know them?"

Reenie started to answer, but then a look of confusion drew her thin, white eyebrows together. "I... shouldn't..." Her voice trailed off vaguely and she shook her head.

Caitlin reached out and touched her hand. "Are you all right, Mrs. Starr?"

Reenie blinked, her eyes cleared, and she gave Caitlin a sunny smile. She covered Caitlin's hand with her own in a surprisingly strong grip. Then she pulled away and reached into her pocket. "I have another good-luck item for you." She tried to pull something out, but it seemed to be too large and bulky. She had to work at it for a moment before it came free. Finally, she held it up.

Caitlin stared. "A bone?"

Reenie beamed and nodded. "I found it on my way over here. I think some dog buried it, then dug it up and forgot about it. Quite fortuitous, I must say, since I knew you'd need it."

Caitlin reached for it and was surprised to find the heavy thing was warm in her hand. She lifted puzzled eyes to Reenie, who smiled.

"A dog's bone," Caitlin said in a flat voice.

"I'm sure you've heard the old saying that even a bad dog can find a good bone sometimes."

"Uh, er, yes, of course," Caitlin responded, though she'd never heard that saying before in her life. Was Reenie saying she was the "bad dog" or that Caitlin was?

"I looked for a horseshoe, but didn't see one, so the bone will have to do. It will teach you another lesson, as the penny and the key chain did." She examined Caitlin keenly. "You did learn something from the penny, didn't you?"

Caitlin blinked and tried to control her amazement at her strange gift. "Learn something?" she asked faintly. She'd certainly learned not to try to convince Reenie that the penny was actually a flattened bottle lid. "Why, yes, I suppose I did," she answered, instead.

Reenie nodded, her floppy-brimmed rain hat bobbing over her eyes. She reached up to push it back. "You learned that wonderful things can happen when you least expect them, and that you have many more friends than you thought you had."

Caitlin thought of her new car, of meeting Jed's family and of her upcoming date with him. "Yes, I did."

"The bone may teach you that what you want isn't always what you should have."

Caitlin thought that was probably asking a great deal of a leftover part from a long-dead cow.

Reenie stood suddenly. The huge fireman's coat engulfed her tiny frame. Her serene face smiled from between the floppy rain hat and the sagging collar of the coat. "Well, it's been nice chatting with you, but I have to go now," she said.

As she started for the door, Caitlin scrambled to her feet. "Let me drive you," she said hurriedly. "The storm is coming and you shouldn't be out on the street—"

"Oh, no, dear," Reenie said. "I'll be perfectly all right."

Caitlin turned and sprinted for the stairs. "Nevertheless, I'll drive you. Please wait right here while I get my keys."

She hurried upstairs to her apartment. She set the bone down on her desk, thought better of it and set it on the floor. She grabbed her keys and purse and dashed out once again. She stopped in the parlor doorway and saw that her guest was gone. Whirling around, she ran to the front door, then down the driveway all the way to the street, calling Reenie's name. But the old woman was gone, as thoroughly as if she'd never been there at all.

Frustrated, Caitlin threw up her hands. "How does she *do* that?"

She turned back toward the house. How could a little old lady disappear so quickly and completely? And so consistently? Worried, Caitlin jumped into her car and made a hurried trip up the highway that led to Crystal Cove, but no sign of Reenie.

Back in her apartment, Caitlin picked up the bone. Reenie said she'd found it on the way over. That meant she'd probably walked by the home of someone who had a dog. All Caitlin had to do to find her was see who had a dog and... But then three-fourths of the people in Crystal Cove had a dog. Maybe she'd have better luck trying to find Reenie through the more usual ways. Caitlin had asked a few people if they knew Reenie, but no one seemed to have seen her, except the people at MacAllen's Market, who said she was an infrequent customer.

The phone rang, startling Caitlin. With the bone still in her hand, she reached for the receiver. When Jed's voice came over the line, she was disconcerted by the thrill of pleasure that shot through her. Her voice was breathless when she said, "Hello, Jed."

"Hi," he responded, then paused. "I called to tell you I think I left the front door unlocked."

"Yes, I know. I took care of it."

"Is something wrong? You sound funny."

There was no way Caitlin was going to tell him that the sound of his voice made her heart hop into her throat. Instead, she looked at her newest good-luck charm again and said, "I'm fine, but I've had another encounter with Reenie Starr."

"Reenie? The old woman from the market? The one who gave you the bottle lid?"

"And the key chain. And now I've got a bone to add to my growing collection."

"Excuse me, did you say 'bone'?"

Caitlin explained Reenie's reasoning, though she couldn't really justify the lady's shaky logic.

"Okay, I think it's official now. You've got the nuttiest guardian angel in heaven, but hey, you can't complain. She's looking out for you. The bottle cap brought you a car," he reminded her. She could hear the smug grin in his voice. "The key chain got you a date with me. What more could a girl want?"

"Humph," she snorted.

"Now, Cait, that's the most unladylike sound I've ever heard you make, unless you count those little sounds you make in the back of your throat when I—"

"Jed!" Heat washed through her, staining her cheeks, and she protested in shock, even though she knew she sounded like someone's maiden aunt.

"Those are more of a purring-cat kind of noise, so I don't think they really count as human sounds, ladylike or otherwise, but they're damned sexy."

In frustration Caitlin banged the bone down on the desktop, nicking the finish. She stared at the mark furiously. "Oh, I wish you would be quiet. I wish you wouldn't talk at all and just listen to me!"

"Sure, Cait," he answered in a tone of pure innocence. "What did you want to say?"

What *did* she want to say? *Don't remind me of what it's like to make love to you?* Who needed a reminder? She thought about it all the time. "Nothing," she finally answered. "Have a safe trip."

"You miss me already," he gloated. "I really am touched. I've got to get Steve's rig on the road. In the meantime, think about our date."

"You wish," she muttered as she hung up, but it was true that she was looking forward to Friday night.

Caitlin ran her knuckles across her forehead. Why was it that when she was with him, she couldn't seem to recall her reluctance to get involved with him? Somehow things like her background, his laid-back attitude, the way his former girlfriends stayed around to look after his welfare didn't seem that important right now.

Obviously she was suffering from some kind of emotional overload. Yeah, that was it. She'd had too much excitement tonight what with the bachelor auction, the visit from Reenie and all. There was only one cure for this problem.

She headed for the kitchen and the pint of cherry-chocolate-cheesecake ice cream that sat waiting in the freezer for exactly this kind of emergency.

CAITLIN DROVE HOME from work the next afternoon feeling pleased with herself, though a little groggy since she hadn't crashed from her self-induced sugar high until after midnight. Still, she felt elated over the day's events. She'd had a stimulating conversation with Geneva Bishop, who had shared the news that there were two new members to her family. Mary had given birth to a boy and a girl. Geneva was thrilled, even if one of the twins was a boy. Caitlin would love to know what had happened to make Ms. Bishop so distrustful of men. Caitlin had reported on the bachelor auction and told Geneva about the odd little woman, Reenie Starr, who seemed to pop up at strange times and places, full of advice. Geneva had surprised Caitlin by suggesting that she listen to the woman. Geneva's statement had been, "You can learn a lot from an old broad."

Caitlin had been amused by this "Genevaism." She'd been on her own so long, she wasn't sure she knew how to take personal advice from others, even from someone as sweet and sincere as Reenie Starr.

However, the whole conversation with Geneva had made Caitlin hopeful. Later in the day, she'd discovered that a mutual fund she'd encouraged some of her clients to invest in was doing better than expected, and it had given her a feeling of satisfaction to know she was responsible for her clients' financial security. Maybe that bone *had* brought her luck.

When she turned into her driveway, Caitlin saw Mr. Mellin's truck beside Terry's in the driveway. With both men working, the house would be finished and on the market by spring, then she would be able to move on with her life. She couldn't imagine why her heart sank at that thought. As she stepped out of the Bel-Air, she heard the high-pitched whine of a power saw.

When she stopped in the hallway to pick up her mail, she saw that Terry was using the saw to cut new decorative moldings for the windows to replace the rain-damaged ones. He turned off the saw when he saw her and flipped the protective goggles to the top of his head. He nodded toward a cellular telephone he'd left on a sawhorse and said, "Jed called. He said he'd be home late tomorrow. He ran into some heavy rain."

"Oh," Caitlin responded. "That's too bad. I..." She paused, not sure what she'd been about to say. The mental image of Jed driving an eighteen-wheeler on slick roads sent shudders of fear rippling up her spine. Surely he wouldn't try it at his usual breakneck speed. "Thanks for telling me, Terry."

Terry pulled his goggles down. "No problem," he said, then gave her an interested look as he added, "He didn't sound too good."

"He didn't?"

"Nah, but it might have been a bad connection. He said for you not to wait up for him."

"I wouldn't have any reason to," she said, though she knew she'd worry about him until he arrived.

Terry grinned. "Yeah, right." He switched on the saw once again, drowning anything further she might have said.

Caitlin rolled her eyes. She didn't know why she bothered to deny it. After her chair-hopping performance on Friday night, everyone in town probably knew there was more than a business partnership between them. She fervently wished she knew what that something was.

The next night, when she finally heard the sound of a car crunching gravel in the driveway, recognized the roar of the powerful engine of Jed's Mustang, relief washed over her.

She waited at the top of the stairs, ready to speak to him as soon as he came up, but the slow, deliberate scrape of his feet on the steps alarmed her. He sounded as if each foot weighed fifty pounds and he had to struggle to lift them.

When she caught sight of him leaning on the banister

as he ascended, Caitlin forgot about her irritation with him and flew down to meet him. One of his arms was laid along the railing, and his head was bent as if he had to summon strength for each step. The brush of her slippers on the stairs caused him to look up.

"Jed! Are you all right?"

"Hi, Cait," he said in a voice that sounded raw and raspy. "How's it going?"

"That's what I'd like to know," she said, hurriedly placing her arm around his waist and propping her shoulder beneath his arm. Heat from his body seared through his shirt and jacket, telling her he was burning up with fever.

"Hey," he responded with a lopsided grin, "this is all right. You're acting like you're actually glad to see me. You've never greeted me like this before. In fact, you're usually ready to throw something at me."

In the muted light of the hallway, she noted his bleary eyes with alarm. "Not tonight," she said, trying to keep the fright out of her voice. "Maybe tomorrow." She reached up to brush his hair out of his face. His feverish skin almost scorched her fingers. "How on earth did you drive an eighteen-wheeler in this condition?" she asked.

"I'm tough," he answered, but he leaned on her gratefully.

"Oh, I can see that," she answered, wrapping both arms around him to keep him steady on his feet.

He gave her another smile, but when he tried to speak, nothing came out. He looked at her in surprise as he mouthed the words, "My voice."

"Maybe this won't be all bad," she muttered, making him frown. "At least you can't boss me around."

"Wanna bet?" he whispered.

Together, they got him upstairs and into his apartment.

Caitlin steered him straight to his bed. He waited, leaning on the bedpost while she turned back the covers, and then he collapsed across the bed as if all his strength had been used in climbing the stairs. He sighed as his eyes closed.

Alarmed anew, Caitlin looked at the way he sprawled bonelessly across the navy blue sheets. She had never seen him like this before. Carefully she sat on the bed, lifted one of his feet and began untying the laces of his sneakers.

He roused enough to mutter, "'S'all right. I'll do that in a minute."

She ignored him, removing his shoes, then tucking him under the covers. He seemed to have fallen asleep, which was probably the best thing for him, but she knew he'd sleep better if she got some aspirin down him.

Caitlin knew there was no aspirin in her apartment, so she searched his bathroom for a bottle, but found none. Finally, feeling like a snoop, she looked in his kitchen, then returned to the bedroom where she located a small bottle in his nightstand, beside a box of condoms.

As soon as she saw it, her gaze flew to his face. Her breath caught, then she exhaled in a sigh of relief when she saw that his eyes were closed and he seemed to be completely unaware of what she was doing. Quietly she removed the bottle of aspirin and closed the drawer. Turning, she hurried to the kitchen for a glass of water.

That box of condoms made her remember the night she'd slept with him, his compelling touch, his gentle humor, the care he'd taken to protect her by using one of those condoms.

Caitlin paused as she filled the glass with water from the tap. Had he used any condoms since that night? Had there been any reason for him to? Since she lived across the hall from him, she was aware of his comings and goings. As far as she knew, none of his frequent female visitors had spent the night with him.

Water filled and overflowed the glass. Hurriedly she turned off the tap, then stood with the dripping glass in her hand. He'd been gone for several nights in the past couple of weeks, though. Could he have met someone?

It was absolutely none of her business. She whipped a towel off the counter, wiped the glass and carried it into the bedroom. With difficulty, she roused Jed long enough to get him to swallow a couple of aspirin and gulp down some water. When he fell back against the pillows, she tugged the covers over him and turned to leave the room.

Her feet slowed to a stop as she approached the doorway. She eased around silently to see that Jed seemed to have fallen instantly asleep, if she could judge by his closed eyes and regular breathing.

How many condoms were in one of those boxes, anyway? It wouldn't hurt to look, she thought. As a consumer, she needed to know information like that. It might be useful someday.

Nonchalantly she wandered back to the bedside, gave Jed another quick peek, then leaned over to open the drawer as silently as possible. With as much stealth as a burglar, she removed the box, checked to see that it was supposed to contain six condoms, then gingerly lifted the lid. There were five foil packages inside. Which meant that if the box had been new when she and Jed had made love all those weeks ago, he hadn't used any since. Elation soared through her and she made a quiet sound of satisfaction. Horrified that she might have awakened Jed, she whipped her head around to see that he was awake and staring at her.

"Strolling down memory lane?" he asked in a raspy

drawl. His dark eyes brightened, but not because of his fever.

Embarrassment flooded Caitlin. She closed the box and dumped it back in the drawer, then slapped it shut. "Certainly not," she said.

Jed grinned. "Nah, not you. You're honest enough to tell me when you want me to make love to you." He nodded toward the nightstand. "Tell you what, why don't you write your name on the ones you want me to use, and as soon as I feel better—"

"Oh, shut up," she said, whipping around and fleeing from the room. She crossed his apartment in quick strides, dashed through the hall and into her own place, closing the door behind her and then bolting it. Her hands flew to her burning cheeks.

What had she been thinking? She had no real interest in how many condoms he used, did she? The number of women he slept with was his business, not hers. Still, she couldn't ignore the satisfaction and elation that she felt knowing the box was still almost full.

JED WAS SICK for three days. Caitlin insisted that he needed to see a doctor. She took it as a sign of how truly terrible he felt when he agreed to let her take him to the clinic. He came home with prescriptions to treat the symptoms of his flu and instructions to stay in bed, rest and drink plenty of fluids.

"Like I didn't already know that," he groused.

"It's better to have a professional opinion," she said in a pedantic tone that hid her relief at knowing he would be well in a day or two.

Once he was back in bed, Caitlin took him bottles of juice, checked his temperature and fed him aspirin for the fever. The next day, his mother came with quarts of chicken soup and news of the newest members of the family. After Laura Bishop assured herself that her younger son was getting better and would be cured with her soup, she left him to sleep and went to Caitlin's apartment. The two of them sat at the small kitchen table, shared a pot of coffee and studied pictures of the newborn twins, who were to be named Susanna and Bradley.

When Jed's mother left, Caitlin again thought of what a warm and generous family he had and wondered if he knew how lucky he was.

By Sunday afternoon she had little to do. She wandered around her apartment for a while, then straightened the items on her desk. She stubbed her toe on something and looked down to see the lucky bone Reenie had given her. Smiling, she turned it in her hands, examining the dirty surface.

Caitlin started to put it down, then decided to show it to Jed. Besides, she should probably heat up some more of the soup his mother had brought him. Carrying the bone, she crossed the hall to find Jed lounging dejectedly on his sofa, morosely leafing through a magazine. When he saw her, his eyes lit up and he leaned back, resting one arm along the back of the sofa and grinning expectantly at her.

Caitlin hid a smile when she saw the eager challenge in his eyes. She didn't think he had his voice back yet, but he had other ways of making his wishes known. Who'd have guessed he could communicate as well without that glib tongue of his? That those dark eyes of his could be so expressive? And so sexy? On second thought, she had to admit she'd already known about the sexy part.

"Hello, Jed. You seem to be feeling better."

He shrugged in response, then gestured for her to sit down.

She handed him the dog bone as she perched in the chair opposite him. "Remember when I told you about Reenie's visit? This is what she gave me. Maybe it'll help you."

He took it from her and gave her a curious look. "Did it do anything for you?" he whispered.

"Not really. I—" She stopped and stared at him, recalling the night of Reenie's visit.

"What?"

Caitlin's eyes widened as she gazed at him, then at the grimy item in his hand. "Nah," she said after a minute, then turned her head and gave him a guilty glance out of the corner of her eye. "Nah," she murmured, shaking her head. "No way."

"What?" he asked again.

"Oh, nothing." She stood suddenly and crossed swiftly to the door. "I'm glad you're feeling better, Jed, I'll—"

"You'll stop right there," he ordered.

Even though the command was whispered, it rocked her to a stop. In an instant he was behind her, his hands were on her shoulders, and he was spinning her around, forcing her to look at him. "'Nah' what?" he demanded. His voice faded out on the last syllable, but it was still insistent.

"Jed, there's nothing to it. Only...my imagination."

"Tell me."

Caitlin breathed a theatrical sigh. "Reenie came by and gave me that thing."

"We've already established that."

Her hands fluttered. "Okay, okay. I took it upstairs and I was holding it when I talked to you on the phone."

He frowned at her, then his brow cleared and his eyes snapped wide open. "And you told me you wished I'd shut up."

"Well, I don't think I said it quite like that," Caitlin answered defensively.

He gaped at her. "You put a curse on me."

"Oh, don't be silly. I did not."

"You *did.* You put a curse on me."

"Don't be ridiculous. I'm not some kind of a witch." Before he could answer, she added, "And neither is Reenie. She's just...different."

He ignored that. "You put a curse on me. Did you do it on purpose?"

She twisted her shoulders, trying to dislodge his hands. "It was a coincidence! The wildest kind of...of chance."

"Like the smashed bottle lid and the call from Gordie and the car?"

Caitlin's mouth opened and closed a couple of times. "Well—"

"And that goofy key chain and the Carlton twins finally losing interest in keeping me from a boring life?"

Caitlin rolled her eyes. "No. That was only some quirk of fate."

"Luck, you mean?" he whispered in a silky tone.

"Yes, all right. Luck." Her eyes flew up to meet his triumphant ones.

"But, Caitlin, you don't believe in luck."

She lifted her chin. "Maybe I've changed my mind."

"And you're willing to admit it, too." His smile grew into a grin. "Cait, my girl, I think you're making progress." His voice seemed to be growing stronger, or maybe it was because she was so close that she could hear him better. He ignored her attempts to escape him, wrapped his arms around her and leaned close. His gray eyes had lightened to silver and his lips were tilted in a devilish smile. "But you owe me a forfeit for putting this curse on me."

"I didn't!" She avoided his lips when they came close to her and fixed him with a severe look. "And stop trying to give me your flu."

"I'm not contagious anymore," he said. "In fact, I'm completely well."

"Who told you that?"

"My mom," he said, blinking innocently. "And I'm sure you realize moms know everything."

"She said that to make you feel better."

"Uh-uh. My mom used to be a Cub Scout den mother. She always tells the truth. Moms are supposed to. Didn't yours?"

Caitlin avoided his eyes and tried to wriggle from his grasp. "Not that I can recall. Jed, why don't you let me go?"

"No." He had gone very still, and for a moment, he looked down into her face with searching intensity before her gaze skittered away. He then pulled her so close a molecule of air couldn't have passed between them. Her belly was pressed up against his, her breasts flattened against his chest. The position was intimate yet playful, and to her shame, arousing. "I like this," he said. "And you do have to pay me a forfeit."

She felt a sizzle of heat stirring, but she managed to tilt her head back and roll her eyes at him dismissively. "I suppose you mean a kiss?"

"Oh, no." His voice broke, then dipped into low tones. "A kiss wouldn't begin to satisfy me." He lowered his head and ran his cheek along the side of her face. "I want something that lasts much longer than that. Something—" he nuzzled behind her ear "—hot and sweet and fulfilling." She shivered. "Something we can both participate in, have fun with." She felt his teeth scrape ever so lightly along her neck. "Something we can draw out until we're both wild with excitement, satisfaction, even joy."

The longer he talked, the more her heart pounded.

"Jed, I... I suppose you mean—" her voice dropped as low as his "—sex."

His smile changed from a wickedly teasing grin to one of such sweetness that her breath was stolen away. "Oh, sweet Caitlin," he whispered. "You are so strong and bold and yet so fearful, and not at all ready for that."

"I'm not?" Her voice trembled with disappointment.

"No, you're not. I rushed you the last time, but I'm not doing it again. When we make love again, you're going to be ready."

She wanted to insist that she was ready now. Instead, she said, "But what about something hot and sweet and...and satisfying?" she asked.

He kissed her lightly on the forehead. "Actually I was thinking of hot chocolate, but keep the other in mind, and I'll get back to you on it."

"Oh, you!" She whirled from his arms and gave him a furious look.

"Don't blame me," he said. "You're the one with sex on the brain."

Her eyes dropped to a noticeable bulge directly below his belt. "Not the only one," she answered.

He turned away from her with a small laugh. "Well, maybe not," he amended. "Now, how about that hot chocolate?"

"I'll make it for you," she said ungraciously, forgetting she had come over in the first place to heat some of Laura's chicken soup for him. She headed for the kitchen, where she found the ingredients she needed and began making the hot beverage. She knew how much he liked to eat, so she wasn't surprised to find a well-stocked pantry, including cocoa and sugar. She could have made hot chocolate in the microwave, but she needed something to keep her busy, so she took a pan from the cupboard to heat the milk on the stove burner.

She was grateful to have something to occupy her because her mind was seething with self-recriminations. Just because Jed talked to her in a slow, sweet, sexy way was no reason for her to let her imagination run away with her. Just because he held her close and she could feel her own arousal, and *his,* didn't mean she should automatically begin having visions of the two of them together, in bed, entwined.

Caitlin's hand shook as she stirred the milk in the pan. It was time for her to face facts. She was far more attracted to Jed than was good for her. All the time she had spent thinking about him these past weeks had only fixed him more firmly in her mind and in her heart. Her plan about thinking of him only ten times a day had long since been blown to the four winds.

When he had come home sick, when he'd needed her, she had been glad to help him. She had felt useful, as if what she was doing for him couldn't be done by anyone else. She had felt important to him.

Even now, when she had virtually volunteered to sleep with him—her face burned at the memory—he had made it clear he wanted something as mundane as hot chocolate. She hadn't felt rejected. Somehow she knew he was easing her toward what he wanted from her. It wasn't simply sex. He wanted the part of her that she had refused to let him see, refused to share with him.

So what was stopping her?

9

"WHAT'S THIS?" CAITLIN asked, glancing at the television as she handed Jed his hot chocolate. She settled on the other end of the sofa with her own. He'd been flipping through the television channels and had decided on something with the grainy appearance of an early seventies made-for-TV movie.

"Science-fiction movie," he said, immediately engrossed. He sipped his drink and made an approving noise. "Thanks."

On the screen a sweet young thing with a body like a young Pamela Lee was parading around in scanty underwear. "I can tell it's science fiction," Caitlin agreed. "No one has a body like that."

"Please notice how I'm keeping my eyes firmly glued to the screen and not letting them stray longingly toward your body while saying, 'Oh yeah?'"

"Duly noted." She squinted at the action on the screen. "Now what's happening?"

"There's a giant spider hiding in her underwear drawer. That's how he gets his jollies. When she opens the drawer, he's going to jump out at her, mad because she's spoiling his fun."

Caitlin set her cup down on the coffee table, propped her feet up beside it and said, "How do you know that?"

"I've seen it before."

The girl was now running bath water. "On purpose?

Or was someone holding you hostage and torturing you by making you watch this?''

"Something like that. It was one afternoon a few years ago while I was baby-sitting Jessica. It's called *Spider World*. I thought it would be educational."

"You mean like 'All about Fungus'?"

Jed chuckled. "Yeah." He set his empty mug beside hers and made himself comfortable by scooting down onto his spine and propping his hands behind his head. "I'll get you up to date on the plot."

"This thing has a plot?" Five minutes later the girl was pouring bath oil into the water. Inside her underwear drawer, a fuzzy black spider with red eyes was peeking coyly through the leg of a pair of her bikini panties.

"Pay attention," Jed instructed. He launched into a story about softball-size rocks from outer space that turned out to actually be radioactive spider eggs. While the unsuspecting citizens of a quiet Arizona town went about their dusty desert days, the spiders plotted to take over the world.

"See?" he said. "They're launching their dastardly plan now. When they hatch, they grow fast." Jed pointed to the screen where another spider, approximately the size of an eighteen-wheeler, was moving at the speed of a slug through town. "That guy only hatched about ten minutes ago."

Citizens were running and screaming, jumping into pickup trucks and speeding away so fast their vehicles overturned in thick tangles of cactus. In one shot a man crawled out of his wrecked truck and began plucking cactus spines from his tongue. Caitlin winced in sympathy.

The spider watched all the action with his malevolent red eyes, then closed them and fell asleep. The panicked townspeople didn't seem to notice.

"Fascinating, isn't it?" Jed asked.

"I think I'd use the word 'stupefying.'" She flapped a hand at the TV. "Look—even the spider is bored to death. Uh, Jed?"

"Yeah?"

"I think I'm having a déjà vu here."

His attention still on the screen, he gestured toward the other room. "Oh? Well, you know where the bathroom is."

She slapped his arm. "I mean I have the feeling I've seen this before."

He turned an admiring look on her. "You mean you like stupid old movies, too?"

"No. I mean this spider reminds me of something. I think it was an art-and-science project we did in first grade. We had to make spiders out of foam balls spray-painted black, with red sequins for eyes and black pipe cleaners for legs."

"Hey, maybe your teacher worked as the special-effects director on this movie," he said, sitting up. "What was her name? We'll look for it when the credits roll."

On the screen, townspeople had returned and were poking the spider with sticks. "Why are they doing that?" she asked.

"They want it to wake up so they can run from it again. I guess they don't get much exercise out there in the desert. Caitlin? What was your teacher's name?"

Mesmerized by the idiocy of this movie, she barely heard him. "I don't remember," she answered. "I went to three different schools that year, so I don't remember which teacher had us do the spiders."

Jed reached for the remote. "Why did you go to three different schools?" he asked, switching the set off. "Was your dad in the military?"

Caitlin blinked and looked up. It took her several seconds to realize what she'd said. Good grief, she hadn't meant to say that. She stood suddenly. "No. No, he wasn't. It was just me and my mom. We moved a lot. Listen, I've got to go. Thanks for the..." She glanced around, unable to remember why she was there. "Whatever," she said. Shaken, she turned toward the door, but stopped and glanced back when the phone rang.

Jed ignored the phone and was beside her in a flash. When she reached for the doorknob, he pressed his hand against the door so she couldn't open it. "Caitlin, what's the matter with you?"

She looked up at his puzzled face. "Nothing. I just remembered something I need to do. At my place."

"What? Hide in the closet?"

She had no answer. They both knew she couldn't come up with an excuse for this behavior. In fact, she wasn't exactly sure why she had reacted to his question with panic. Old habits died hard. Confused, she shook her head at him, not sure what to say.

Jed had no such problem. He took her by the hand and led her back to the sofa, but before he reached it, the phone rang again. He gave it a distracted look. "I'd let the answering machine pick it up, but it might be Steve or Mary needing something. Then you and I are going to talk. And don't argue. I'm not a well man. If you argue, I might have a relapse." As if he was afraid she'd take off if he let go of her, he pulled her with him to the desk where he picked up the receiver.

"Hello?"

Faintly Caitlin could hear a woman's voice on the other end. It wasn't his sister-in-law. This woman's voice was deep and sultry. Deciding instantly that she really didn't want to be where she was, Caitlin attempted to pull away, but he reeled her back.

Jed shot a swift, uncomfortable glance at Caitlin as he answered. "Hi, Maria. How's it going? Oh? Where did you hear that? No, I've got a touch of the flu." He faked a cough and Caitlin rolled her eyes at him. This was the first she'd heard of a cough.

Jed smirked at her, then paused to listen. As he did so, Caitlin tried to twist her wrist from his grasp, but he stopped her by pulling her arm behind her back and bringing her close. He held her firmly as he spoke into the receiver. "That's sweet of you, honey, but not necessary. My mom's been here with her chicken soup."

Caitlin was close enough now to hear Maria say, "I could come over and heat some for you."

His eyes glinted wickedly as he met Caitlin's eyes. "Thanks, but my neighbor's here. She's keeping things plenty hot."

Caitlin's eyes widened and she aimed the heel of her sneaker at his bare toes, but he bent at the waist, dragging her feet off the floor. Outraged, she dangled in midair. "Let go of me, Jed," she demanded, but he ignored her.

"Is that your neighbor?" Maria asked, then her voice cooled. "Oh, the one who bid for you at the bachelor auction? She made quite a spectacle of herself."

"She's nuts about me," he said.

"In your dreams," Caitlin said, trying to wriggle from his grasp.

Realizing he was about to lose his grip on her, Jed spoke hastily. "Thanks for calling, Maria. I've got to go. My hands are full." While Maria was still speaking, he hung up, wrapped both arms around Caitlin and frogmarched her back to the couch. He tossed her down on it and gave her a ferocious look that seemed to nail her in place.

Jed pointed a finger at her nose. "We're not going to do this anymore," he said.

"Do what?" she asked warily.

"This business of your secret life."

"My secret life?"

"We've known each other for almost three months. We've lived across the hall from each other, become business partners, lovers, and I *thought* we were friends. I have lots of friends, but not one like you. For some reason you seem to think I can't be trusted. You hoard information about yourself like it was gold. Are you a participant in the federal witness-protection program? Hiding out from a Chinese tong? From your family? What gives?"

Caitlin had never seen him so angry. In fact, she'd never seen him angry at all. It slowly dawned on her that he was furious because she had hurt him. She didn't know what to say. She couldn't defend her actions, because she knew he was right. Now somehow it didn't seem that important to keep her secrets anymore. Hadn't she been thinking that while she was in the kitchen?

"Jed," she began, "I wouldn't be hiding out from my family. I don't have one. I don't have anyone."

His hands lifted to rest at his waist. He frowned as he looked into her eyes. "Cait, everyone has someone."

"No, they don't. I don't."

"Tell me about it," he said, sitting down beside her on the sofa.

Her hands clenched together in her lap, but he reached down and pried her fingers apart, holding her hands in his. He lifted his chin at her as if urging her to go on.

She took a deep breath. "I know you think I'm too

focused on work, on providing for my future. I don't believe in luck because, until I started providing for myself, took control of my own life, I didn't seem to have anything but *bad* luck.''

His anger had faded away, replaced by compassion. "How long have you been providing for yourself?"

"Since I was sixteen. That was when my mother abandoned me." Caitlin looked away and stared at a painting over his desk. It was of a ship on a storm-tossed sea being beckoned to port by the beam from a lighthouse.

"Abandoned you? You mean, she walked off and left you?"

"That's right."

"But...but mothers don't do that." Horror rose in his voice.

Caitlin raised an eyebrow.

"Well, I guess they do," he said, shaking his head.

"Yes, and in a way, I was grateful to her for it."

"Why would you be grateful?"

"I was grateful she didn't do it sooner. My younger life wasn't anything great, believe me, but at least she kept me with her. My mother had me when she was fifteen. She was a runaway, probably didn't know who my father was. At least, it's not listed on my birth certificate. We lived all over California. Usually left one city or another one jump ahead of the law." For a moment Caitlin felt the confusion and fear she'd known as a child wash over her. She must have shivered because Jed pulled her closer and tucked her head under his chin. His arms enfolded her in a cocoon of safety she couldn't remember ever feeling before.

"Go on," he urged. "You've come this far."

"Jed, she was an alcoholic, a sometime drug user, a petty thief—and a prostitute, and not necessarily in that order. I didn't know what a prostitute was until I was about nine and one of my friends, I think we were in San Diego then, couldn't come home to play with me because her mom said mine was a hooker. I didn't know what that was. When I found out, I realized why there were always so many men around our place. Anyway, one day, when I was sixteen, I came home from school to find that almost everything was gone from the cheap little apartment we'd been renting. Weeks later she wrote from Las Vegas, said she was sorry. Anyway, the rent was paid for the month, so I got a job working as a waitress and I stayed. It was a scramble.''

She stopped for a moment and pulled back to look at his face. Above all, she didn't want him to feel sorry for her or to think she'd done it all on her own. "People were kind," she said. "Tony Danova, the owner of the restaurant where I worked, let me take food home. When I was a senior, he and his wife, Anna, paid for my senior pictures. They bought my prom dress, too, and took pictures of me wearing it." She smiled at the memory.

"It's good you had someone, but..." Jed's voice faltered. "Your mother dumped you when you were *sixteen?*" Now his voice had a tone she'd never heard him use before. Puzzled, Caitlin looked up and saw rage simmering in his eyes. "Why would she have done something like that?"

"She had a new boyfriend who didn't want a kid around, though I wasn't much of a kid at sixteen, but she chose him, instead of me." Caitlin freed one hand from the confining afghan and touched Jed's face. "I don't begrudge her that. In fact, I was glad. It meant I didn't have to worry about her anymore, make excuses for her, cover for her—clean up after her, dodge her drunken boyfriends. Maybe it was selfish of me, but I could finally concentrate on myself, on getting what I wanted." She gave him a lopsided smile. "And what I wanted was stability—emotional, mental and financial."

"Didn't the court step in?"

"They didn't know. No one knew for a long time." She winced. "I'm not proud of this, but whenever I needed my mother's signature on something for school, I forged it. I had goals, you see. I couldn't get mixed up with the child-welfare system. They would have gotten in my way, tried to put me in foster care, do what was 'best' for me, but I *knew* what was best for me—being an honor student, getting a scholarship, an education, a career that would give me security."

Jed stared at her, feeling humbled and ashamed. He'd known she was smart and her beauty was obvious. He hadn't realized she was a self-made woman. In fact, he'd never known the truth of that phrase until now.

"My mother died a few years ago. Cirrhosis of the liver. She was thirty-six years old. Her life hadn't amounted to anything." Caitlin lifted her head and Jed saw the sadness in her eyes change to determination. "I'm not going to be like that," she said firmly. "I'm *not*."

"No, you won't." He caught her hand and pressed his lips to it. "Caitlin, I think you're my hero." He shook his head. "I wish I'd known some of this before."

She pulled away and gave him a look that of weary resignation. "Jed, do you really think that someone who's been on her own for as long as I have finds it easy to confide in others?"

His eyes narrowed as he looked down at her. "I think you confide in my aunt Geneva."

"Not this stuff," Caitlin said. "Only things about you. Besides, that's different."

"Because she's a woman?"

"A wise, elderly woman," Caitlin said. "And they're long-distance confidences, if you know what I mean. It's harder to say things, personal things, face-to-face."

Which told him exactly how much it meant that she'd confided in him. "I guess it is."

When he touched her face, he was amazed to see that his hand was shaking. For an easygoing guy with a laid-back attitude toward relationships, responsibilities, to life in general, he was suddenly feeling a ton of obligations, all of them to this slim chestnut-haired woman who seemed to know so much about strength.

He understood now. He understood why security was so important to her, why she hated the time that had been wasted the past few weeks on the renovations of this house, why she'd been so embarrassed by the television ad where he'd kissed her publicly and by the photograph and article in the paper. Even though those things had turned out well, it must have been difficult for her because they had brought her the kind of attention she didn't want. He wished now that he'd understood, but how could he when she hadn't told him?

It was time for him to make up for past mistakes. He cupped her cheek with his hand and tilted her face up to his.

Caitlin looked into Jed's eyes and saw something there she hadn't seen before. Along with the compassion she'd already noted was tenderness.

"I want to make love to you, Caitlin."

Her heart began a slow, steady beat that seemed to pulse from her toes to her hairline. "You...you do?"

"It'll be different this time," he said.

She reached for him, signaling that she was ready for him at last to make love to her. As naturally and effortlessly as if she'd done this a hundred times, Caitlin wound her arms around his neck and brought her lips to his. "I know," she said.

His mouth came down on hers, fierce with need. He stood, pulled her into his arms and carried her to his bed.

Caitlin heard the mattress sigh, felt it give beneath her as Jed set her down on it, then swiftly removed his clothes to lie beside her.

Caitlin looked into his face, at his eyes sheltered by his thick brows, the set of his jaw, his gently smiling lips. The last time, they'd made love in a rush of heat, influenced by champagne, by elemental needs. Those needs were still there, but this time they were making love with a consciousness that had been missing the first time.

Caitlin's eyes drifted almost shut and through the screen of her lashes she could see the intensity in his face. Her heart overflowed with warmth and tenderness when she realized he was trying to make this as memorable and wonderful as he could.

He was succeeding beyond his sincerest expectations.

When Jed's hands touched her, they were as soft as the her sweater, which he eased over her head. He lifted one strap over her shoulder and down, then the other. He swept her bra aside, then paused to look at her. His eyes glittered.

"You are so beautiful, Caitlin."

His earnest voice made her believe she was beautiful in a way she never had before. Caitlin relaxed and felt the heat and tension build as his hands skimmed over her skin. His hands were followed by his lips, which took their time in exploring the soft texture of her throat. Caitlin arched her neck with a husky moan.

"There you go again," Jed murmured. "Making those noises that drive me wild."

She gave a breathy laugh. "Do you want me to stop?"

"Hell, no," he murmured, moving to her shoulder. "I don't ever want you to stop. In fact—" his mouth moved to the swell of her breast "—I want to hear it often, nightly, in fact, for years."

Fear shivered through her. "Jed, I don't think that's such a good—" His mouth found the peak of her nipple and her objection exploded in a blast of heat. Her fingers dug into his shoulders. "Jed!"

He trailed kisses to her other breast. "Tell me that you belong to me, Cait," he whispered.

Her hands skimmed down his arms, then up again to cup his face. "What?" she asked against his lips.

He looked into her eyes. "I said, I want you to say you belong to me, as I belong to you."

"Jed, I don't know." Her voice caught. "I've never belonged anywhere, and—"

"Forget about that. You belong to me. We belong together."

The word "belong" seared into her brain. Was it true? She couldn't think clearly with his mouth on hers, his hands on her, readying her for his possession.

It seemed so right, as if she did belong to him, as if all the wanderings and upsets of her life had somehow brought her here, to this moment, to this man. But saying what he wanted her to say was such a big step she didn't know if she could do it.

"Never mind, Caitlin," he said after a moment. He lifted himself away from her and looked into her eyes. Even in the shadows, she could see compassion and tenderness there. "It'll come."

Her throat clogged with gratitude as he said it. Her arms came up and around him, holding him tight. She kissed him, caressed him, showing him with her body what her mouth couldn't seem to speak.

When she did so, the heat between them built even further. Her body begged for fulfillment. He responded, giving her what she asked with whispered murmurs, arousing touches and finally by sinking himself deep inside her.

Caitlin arched upward, her hips lifting to take him in. She gasped as he began to move in a slick, sensual, satisfying dance that brought them both to the peak. When it hit, her eyes flew open to see him above her, his face set, his eyes full of joyous tenderness. Sensation crashed through her, colors exploded in her head, and his prophetic statement came true. She did belong to him.

DID SHE REALIZE what she'd done? Jed wondered. He couldn't move away from her yet. He couldn't break that bond, but he didn't think she realized how strongly they'd forged one between them. Once she started to think about it, she would worry. In fact, she might panic. She was too quick to figure things out once she started thinking.

Jed thought it might be a damned good idea if neither of them did much thinking right now. He lowered his mouth to hers and began the arousing dance once again.

Caitlin moaned when his mouth settled on her breast. "Jed?"

"Relax, honey," he said. "We've been waiting a long time for this night. Let's make the most of it."

He could feel her wanting to protest, could almost see the words forming on her lips, so he sealed them inside her by placing his lips on hers. "There's a time for talk," he murmured. "But this isn't it. At least not yet."

This time, there was no more hesitation, no more resistance. To his joy, he saw she was smiling. "Yes, Jed," she said.

He returned to the pleasure of driving them both wild.

Caitlin wrapped herself around him and joined him in the journey.

CAITLIN AWOKE TO FIND Jed's arm around her, his leg entwined with hers. A glance at his bedside clock told her it was still two hours before she had to begin preparing for work.

She lay with her arm hugging Jed's and tried to analyze her tangle of feelings. There was fear, but she couldn't quite determine its source because it didn't feel like what she'd experienced when she'd awakened with Jed all those weeks ago. She was touched by tenderness and warmth for him, and she wasn't as worried. That *had* to be progress.

She didn't think she had moved, but Jed's arm tightened around her and he spoke into her hair. "You think too much."

She smiled. "How can a person think too much?"

"I don't know many people who can do *any* thinking at this hour of the morning, but if anyone can manage it, you can." He shifted and turned them both so that they lay thigh to thigh, belly to belly. "Don't think," he said, and she could almost hear the smile in his voice as he said, "Just feel."

And feel she did. Caitlin felt his hands smoothing over her body, his mouth on hers, his body pressing down on her, into her. He was gentle, he was rough, he made her want to laugh and to weep. When he brought her to the peak of fulfillment, she gasped and cried out, then lay limp in his arms.

After several long minutes Caitlin opened languorous eyes and focused on him. The sun was coming up, its first rays stealing across the room so that she could see his face. His hair was tousled from her hands, his lips as swollen from kisses as hers were, his dark eyes so serious and steady that wariness had her pulling away to look at him. "Looks like *you're* doing some thinking now."

"I am."

She didn't like the heaviness of his tone. "What, Jed? What is it?"

"We didn't get our Friday-night date," he said slowly. "In fact, none of this has worked out the way I'd planned."

"Exactly what had you planned?" His expression made her nervous because she couldn't read it. Was it regret?

"I didn't expect to get sick."

"No one ever does."

"No, but I thought when we made love again it would be the usual," he admitted with a shrug. "Dinner, theater." His smile flickered. "Seduction."

His tone, the solemn look in his eyes so unlike him that a chill swept through her. She edged further away from him. She didn't like what he was saying, either. "The usual?"

"Yes." His voice was low, his words hesitant as if he was sorting them before speaking. "I thought it would be so easy, that the one night we spent together weeks ago wasn't anything unusual, that if we did this—" his hand swept down her body "—it would be great for a while, then I could turn you into a friend like…"

"Like all the other women in your life," Caitlin finished for him. Clearly it was regret she was seeing and hearing. Hurt blossomed and she spoke before she thought, but hating the cynicism in her tone. "I'm not surprised. That's what I expected to happen, too. You're good at it."

"Good at it?" he asked, staring at her. "Good at what?"

Caitlin pulled away completely and he let her go. "Good at keeping your former girlfriends as friends, at continuing to take care of them. You said yourself it's because you were responsible for your sister. It's a habit you've developed." Caitlin reached for the sheet, but he was lying on top of it. When she tugged at it, he scooted away from her so she could cover herself. She gave him a smile as brittle as old parchment. "But you don't have to worry about me. I don't need you to take care of me. I've always taken care of myself, remember?" Sickness rolled in her throat and she felt as if she was suffocating, but she struggled on. "You don't have to worry about me hanging around, knitting sweaters for you, bringing you brownies from the bakery, or…or making you the featured sexy hunk in a book I'm writing."

Jed's eyes grew stormy as he listened to this little speech. "You know, if you'd let me finish what I'm trying to say—"

"There's no need," she said. "I'm not going to be an albatross around your neck. We're neighbors, business partners. This—" her hand swept out to indicate the bed and the two of them "—was fun, but don't feel like you have to repeat it."

"Repeat it?" He stared at her. "Have you listened to a single word I've said either last night or today?"

She didn't want to burst into tears, but she didn't know how much longer she could keep from it. How had all this gone so wrong? She glanced around, looking for her clothes. Escape was uppermost in her mind. Escape before she indulged in pure humiliation. "Well," she answered in a vague tone, "people say things they don't mean, and—"

"I don't!" Jed rolled off the bed and stood glaring at her. After a few seconds, he turned and sifted through the covers they'd tossed from the bed to find her jeans and sweater. He handed them to her.

Her hands trembled as she took the items from him. They dropped from her hands, fluttering down like her damaged dreams. "Jed, I—"

"I don't know what kind of man you think I am, Caitlin, but you've lived across the hall from me for months now. I thought we knew each other. I thought we were friends. I thought you'd know this wasn't just sex."

Caitlin stared at him, waiting for him to say that it was love, but the words didn't come. And she couldn't seem to form the words herself.

Jed turned away and picked up his own clothes. "I'm going into the kitchen to make coffee while you get dressed. Then we're going to talk about this." He turned and strode from the room.

10

CAITLIN LIFTED HER HAND as if to stop him, but then she grabbed her clothes and hurried into them. While he was in the kitchen, she scurried past him and dashed for the front door. She heard him call her name, but she kept running, whirling inside her own apartment and closing the door. Then she leaned against it and fought for breath.

She loved him. That was why this was so terrible. She loved him and he wanted to turn her into one of his drop-by-and-check-on-Jed friends. Caitlin's hands clasped together at her waist. She couldn't do that because she realized now she'd been in love with him for weeks, probably since the day he'd walked into her office with his killer grin.

Her eyes full of distressed tears, Caitlin stared blindly at the clock and saw it was time for her to get ready for work. Sure, she could do that, she thought as she pushed away from the door, stumbling slightly as she did so. She would concentrate on work until she could decide exactly what she was going to do.

She hurried through her preparations for work, barely noticing what she was doing because her mind was consumed with Jed, with her feelings and reactions. She needed help or direction of some kind, but didn't know who to ask. Her best friends, Tony and Anna, were in San Francisco. She could ask them, but it seemed unfair after weeks of not contacting them to suddenly spring this problem on them. Besides, she'd always kept her own counsel. Her friends would be flabbergasted if she called and asked for advice on her love life.

She couldn't ask anyone. She had to work this out for herself. That decided, Caitlin grabbed up her briefcase and purse and headed for the door. As she reached for the knob, she heard heavy footsteps in the hall. At first she felt a moment of panic, but then she realized it couldn't be Jed. It sounded like this person was wearing boots. Maybe Terry had come to work early.

She jumped when the visitor rapped on her door. Cautiously, she opened it to see a tall figure clad entirely in black. He was facing away from her, but when he turned around, her jaw dropped.

"Jed?"

Her bewildered gaze traveled over him. He hadn't shaved, so his jaw was shadowed with the beginnings of his beard. His hair was slicked back, and he wore a black T-shirt, black leather jacket and pants and heavy biker's boots.

"Come on," he said, reaching out and grabbing her wrist. He plucked her purse and briefcase from her hands and dropped them inside the door, then closed it.

"Jed!" she protested, trying to pull away as he dragged her out into the hall. "What are you doing?"

"Something I should have done months ago," he growled, his face so grim.

"Whatever this is better not include violence," she said.

"It should, but it won't." He pulled her into his apartment, closed the door and locked it. There was another lock near the top she had never noticed before. He locked this one with a key and slipped it into the pocket of his skin-tight leather pants. At any other time she would have taken a moment to admire how beautifully those pants hugged his powerful thighs and terrific tush, but right now she was too stunned to do anything except gape at him.

"Why are you doing this? And why are you wearing those clothes?"

"To show you that the days of Mr. Nice Guy are over."

"They are?"

"Yup," he said, advancing on her. "No more Mr. Nice Guy."

She backed away, her golden-brown eyes wide and wary. "O...kay," she said, trying to humor him. "Why no more Mr. Nice Guy?"

"Because I'm going to prove to you that I don't intend to treat you like all the other women in my life—not that there are that many," he added in a tone of righteous indignation. He lifted his hand and counted them off on his fingers. "My mother, my sisters, my aunt, a few friends." He wiggled his thumb at her. "That leaves room for you. Take off your jacket."

"Room for...? What?"

He put his hands on his hips and stuck out his jaw. "I said take off your jacket. It's ugly, anyway."

Caitlin had never seen him like this. Where was the laid-back fun guy she knew? Oh, yes—no more Mr. Nice Guy. She looked down at her sensible brown-and-black pin-striped suit jacket. Well, okay, maybe it wasn't her most attractive, but it wasn't ugly. She lifted her head. "Jed, why would I want to take off my... Oh!" He'd stepped forward and stripped it from her arms.

He strode to the bathroom with it dangling from his hand, and a few moments later she heard the shower running. She scurried after him and arrived at the very moment he tossed it into the tub.

"Jed!" she shrieked. "Have you gone crazy?"

"Yeah. Now your skirt."

"I'm not taking off my skirt so you can ruin it by throwing it into the shower!" she shouted. Her amazement was finally giving way to anger. Who did he think he was, anyway?

He shrugged. "Okay. *I'll* do it."

When he reached for her, she tried again to pull away, but he was a man with a purpose. He had her out of her skirt in less than ten seconds despite her struggles. He tossed it into the shower along with the jacket. "Now your blouse."

Caitlin was learning. She skimmed out of it in record time and threw it at him. "That's as far as I go," she said, standing before him in her underwear. "Until I find out what's going on here."

"Panty hose," he said in disgust. "Those, too."

"No!"

"Yes." He started toward her.

"Okay, okay." She took them off and he snagged them, one-handed, from the air as she threw them at his head. They went into the trash. He cranked the shower off, grabbed her hand and hauled her into his bedroom.

"Jed," she said, sawing back on her arm. "If you think we're going to solve this with sex…"

"No. I tried that already. In fact, I tried it twice and it didn't work because you wake up the next morning thinking you know everything and won't even listen to me. We're not doing that again," he said, stabbing a finger at her. Turning, he grabbed something from the bed and handed it to her.

Caitlin blinked. It was a set of biker clothes like his. Leather pants, jacket, black T-shirt.

"These were my sister Diana's," he told her. "Put them on."

"Are you kidding?" She knew she'd wasted her breath as soon as she said it. The determination in his face told her he wasn't. She grabbed the T-shirt and slipped it over her head and then began struggling into the pants, which were too small. Diana must be a tiny woman, she decided as she worked them up her hips and struggled with the zipper. "Now, will you tell me what this is all about?"

Seemingly satisfied that she was doing what he wanted, he picked up a pair of boots and some socks and gave them to her. When she was completely dressed, he said, "I've got a secret life and no one has ever shared it with me before."

"A secret life?"

"Yup." Some of his irritation with her seemed to be fading and a silvery glow of anticipation began shining in his eyes. "I've got a Harley Fatboy parked in a shed behind my dad's garage. We're going for a ride down the coast highway. No one's been on that bike with me since Diana moved to Sacramento. You're the first."

She met his eyes and a smile started to form. "Why me?"

"That's what I was trying to tell you a while ago when you ran off." He paused, took a breath and went on, "This didn't turn out like I'd planned because I've fallen in love with you."

"You have?" Caitlin asked softly.

"I can't treat you like all my other old girlfriends because I don't want you to *be* an old girlfriend. I want you to be my wife."

"You do?" A blend of amazement and joy clogged any more words she might have said.

Jed waited a second, an edge of uncertainty slipping into his face. "Well, how about it?"

Maybe she couldn't speak, but she could move. Caitlin rushed into his arms. "Yes," she managed. "Yes."

He swept her up and kissed her, long and slow. Breathless, she pulled away, her eyes shining with tears. "I didn't know that I loved you until this morning."

"Better late than never," he growled, and kissed her again. "So, when will you marry me?"

"Anytime you say."

He grinned. "An easy woman. I like that. What about a honeymoon?"

Her eyes glinted with mischief. "Anywhere you say."

He rewarded her with another kiss. "Can I drive your car?"

Caitlin came up on the toes of her biker boots, wrapped her arms around his neck, planted a long, hard kiss on him and said, "Not on your life."

THEY WERE MARRIED in November in the little church Jed's family had attended for forty years. It seemed that half of Crystal Cove was there, and even more came to the reception at the community center.

Caitlin's dress was the kind young girls dream of, with yards of white satin and lace trailing behind her. Her practical soul had balked at the expense, but the romantic nature growing in her said that she would only be marrying once, so she'd better do it up in style. Her friends had come from San Francisco, Tony Danova to give her away and wife Anna to be her matron of honor. Jessica Bishop was her only bridesmaid.

For the reception Jed had hired a three-piece band, who were set up at the end of the basketball court. The group only seemed to play fast numbers, which the guests liked. Even Steve and Mary were dancing, though not in time to the zippy music. They were each holding a twin as they glided around the edge of the big room.

Caitlin smiled at them as they moved past, then grinned at her own husband, who was holding her close while trying to execute a complicated series of steps. He took her hand and spun her in a twirl. "Is this an actual dance," she asked through her laughter, "or are you making this up as you go along?"

"Well, you know I'm an impromptu kind of guy," he said. "And besides, if I keep you moving fast enough, no one else will try to cut in and dance with you. I have no intention of sharing you with anyone."

They whizzed past his parents, who were sitting this one out. Caitlin waved as they passed in a blur. "You married me under false pretenses. I thought you were laid-back, easygoing."

"Not if there's a chance someone might try to make a move on my wife."

"I think you're overreacting. Besides, I'm getting dizzy." By digging in her heels, she managed to slow him down. "Why don't we get some punch?"

With a good-natured shrug, he grabbed her hand and parted a way through the crowd. It took a while because they were stopped so often by well-wishers.

Jed had his hand at her waist, guiding her along, when he spoke in her ear. "Hey, look, there's my aunt Geneva."

Caitlin craned her neck to see. "You're kidding. Where?"

"Right where we're headed—over by the punch bowl. Mom says she was at the ceremony, but she refused to come through the reception line. She says those things take too long. I'm supposed to bring you over to meet her."

"Well, let's go," she said, eagerly pulling him along. She couldn't wait to meet her mentor, the woman who'd sent so much business her way and given her such valuable advice.

Geneva Bishop turned out to be tall and rangy, like the rest of the Bishops. She had short white hair and steady gray eyes. She shook Caitlin's hand and smiled her approval. "You've done well, Jed."

Jed lifted an eyebrow at her and smiled. "High praise from you, Aunt Geneva. I'm flattered."

"Don't be," she said repressively. "It was meant as a compliment for Caitlin."

"I should have known." He hugged Caitlin closer. "Compliment her all you want, Auntie. It won't turn her head. She's too smart to be affected by your effusive flattery."

"She *is* smart," a voice said from behind Geneva. "Smart enough to keep you in line."

Caitlin and Jed looked and their mouths dropped open as Reenie Starr stepped up with a cup of punch. "Hello, dear," she said. "I'm so happy for both of you." She glanced around. "This is a lovely reception."

"Mrs. Starr!" Jed said.

"Reenie!" Caitlin exclaimed.

"The very same," she said, her eyes twinkling. "You knew I'd come to your wedding, didn't you?"

Jed lifted his hand and rubbed his jaw. "To tell you the truth, we thought you were a ghost or a witch or something from that way you have of disappearing so fast."

She shook her head. "I only disappeared fast when you offered help. I didn't need it. I like being independent."

"That's the way you'll be when you're old, Caitlin," Geneva said, and smiled at Reenie.

"Do you two know each other?" Caitlin asked.

"Since we were children, though I moved away from here when I was a young girl," Reenie answered. "Geneva and I met by chance in Los Angeles a few months ago and got reacquainted."

Caitlin stared at the two of them, then spoke to Geneva. "How come you didn't tell me you knew her when I told you about her on the phone?"

Geneva's gray eyes sparkled as she took a sip of her punch. "Because she's hiding out from her children, of course."

"They want to put me in a *home*," Reenie said, outraged. "They think I can't take care of myself because sometimes I get a little addled. When I met Geneva again and told her about it, she offered to let me come stay in the little apartment behind her house for a while."

"Well, I'll be dam...darned," Jed said. "When you said you lived down Old Barton Road, you really *did*." He looked at his aunt. "And that's why you told the family to stay away from your place."

"None of you needed to be nosing around there, anyway," Geneva answered with a sniff. "And Reenie needed some time alone to prove she'd be all right."

"Yes," Reenie confirmed. "I kept to myself and took care of myself so my children would see I can still be on my own. I call and check in with them every once in a while."

Caitlin and Jed exchanged laughing glances. "Well," Caitlin said, "I'm glad to know you weren't a figment of my imagination."

"I'm solid, all right." Reenie reached out to grip Caitlin's hand firmly. "See? And I recognized you the first time we met because I'd seen your picture in the brochure Jed sent Geneva. She'd told me all about you, and when I moved up here, we kept each other up-to-date." She and

Geneva exchanged smiles like a couple of conspirators. "And I knew you didn't believe in luck because your brochure said so. 'Hard work and knowledge are what build a successful portfolio,'" she quoted.

"Oh." Caitlin blinked. She gave Jed an apologetic smile. "I see now. When I told Geneva things about Jed, she told you, and you came to talk to me about him."

"That's right. Geneva and I felt you needed some wise counsel. After all, she's been dealing with the men in the Bishop family for a long time. She knows how difficult they can be."

Jed shook his head as he took this in. "So you were looking out for Caitlin all along."

"Yes, but I don't think there was really any need. She's managed well for herself," Geneva answered.

"There's one more thing," Reenie said. "I'm the owner of that old farm on Barton Road you've been trying to buy for so long. My maiden name is Barton. The farm belonged to my father, but it failed during the depression and no one ever tried to farm that land again. I didn't want to see the property spoiled by a big development of condominiums and golf courses, but if you still want to buy it, I'll sell it to you."

Caitlin felt Jed give a start. "Why, I—"

"There's one condition, though," she broke in. "You and Caitlin must build yourselves a home there, one to share with your children when they come along."

Caitlin looked up at Jed, who opened his mouth, then closed it again. He seemed stunned. She'd never seen him at a loss for words, so she spoke for both of them. "Thank you, Reenie. That's exactly what we'll do."

She beamed at them. "Perfect."

Geneva touched her friend on the arm. "Why don't you come along and meet the other members of our family?

Since you're going to be staying with me for a while, you'll want to get to know them." The two women melted into the crowd.

Jed gaped after them. "You know what this means?"

Caitlin placed her arm around his waist. "It means we'll have a house on some lovely property."

"Yeah," he said in a strangled voice. "Right up the road from my aunt. She'll want to baby-sit, you know."

"That's okay."

"That's what you think," he said, giving her a horrified look. "Whenever she baby-sat for us when we were little, she made Steve and me join our sisters for tea parties!"

Caitlin burst out laughing. "She was only trying to erase your gender bias."

"You sound exactly like her." He grabbed two cups of punch from the table and handed one to her, then clinked his cup against hers and encouraged her to drink up. "There's only one thing to do," he announced when he'd drained his cup.

"What's that?"

"Figure out some way to make sure we only have girls! I'm strong enough to hold my own against all you women, but I'm not going to wish it on a son."

With that said, he whisked the cup from her hand and whirled her onto the dance floor again. Caitlin went gladly, eager to take on the challenge of their life together. She'd chosen well, she thought: a hometown, a home, Jed Bishop to love, someday children of her own. Who needed wishes or luck?

COMING NEXT MONTH

MILLS & BOON®
Enchanted™

THE OUTBACK AFFAIR by Elizabeth Duke

Natasha was horrified when her tour guide turned out to be Tom Scanlon—the man who'd once jilted her. It was too intimate a situation for ex-lovers—but Tom wanted Natasha back. And now he had two weeks alone with her to prove just how much!

THE BEST MAN AND THE BRIDESMAID by Liz Fielding

As chief bridesmaid, Daisy is forced out of her usual shapeless garb and into a beautiful dress. Suddenly the best man, determinedly single Robert Furneval, whom she has always loved, begins to see her in a whole new light...

HUSBAND ON DEMAND by Leigh Michaels

Jake Abbott has arrived at his brother's house—to discover that Cassie has been hired to look after the residence. He's clearly very happy for their temporary living arrangements to become more intimate. But what about permanent...?

THE FEISTY FIANCÉE by Jessica Steele

When Yanice fell for her boss, Thomson Wakefield, she adhered to her belief that love means marriage, but did it mean the same for him? A near tragic accident brings her answer, but can Yanice trust the proposal of a man under heavy sedation?

Available from 3rd March 2000

Available at most branches of WH Smith, Tesco, Martins, Borders, Easons, Volume One/James Thin and most good paperback bookshops

For the incurable romantic

MILLS & BOON®

Enchanted™

Warm and tender novels that let you experience the magic of falling in love.

Eight brand new titles each month.

Available at most branches of WH Smith, Tesco, Martins, Borders, Easons, Volume One/James Thin and most good paperback bookshops

MILLS & BOON®

By Request™

Three bestselling romances brought back to you by popular demand

Latin Lovers

The Heat of Passion by *Lynne Graham*
Carlo vowed to bring Jessica to her knees, however much she rejected him. But now she faced a choice: three months in Carlo's bed, or her father would go to jail.

The Right Choice by *Catherine George*
When Georgia arrived in Italy to teach English to little Alessa, she was unprepared for her uncle, the devastating Luca. Could she resist?

Vengeful Seduction by *Cathy Williams*
Lorenzo wanted revenge. Isobel had betrayed him once—now she had to pay. But the tears and pain of sacrifice had been price enough. Now she wanted to win him back.

Available at branches of WH Smith, Tesco, Martins, Borders, Easons, Volume One/James Thin and most good paperback bookshops

FREE!

2 Books
and a surprise gift!

We would like to take this opportunity to thank you for reading this Mills & Boon® book by offering you the chance to take TWO more specially selected titles from the Enchanted™ series absolutely FREE! We're also making this offer to introduce you to the benefits of the Reader Service™—

- ★ FREE home delivery
- ★ FREE gifts and competitions
- ★ FREE monthly Newsletter
- ★ Books available before they're in the shops
- ★ Exclusive Reader Service discounts

Accepting these FREE books and gift places you under no obligation to buy; you may cancel at any time, even after receiving your free shipment. Simply complete your details below and return the entire page to the address below. **You don't even need a stamp!**

YES! Please send me 2 free Enchanted books and a surprise gift. I understand that unless you hear from me, I will receive 4 superb new titles every month for just £2.40 each, postage and packing free. I am under no obligation to purchase any books and may cancel my subscription at any time. The free books and gift will be mine to keep in any case.

NOEB

Ms/Mrs/Miss/Mr ....Initials..

BLOCK CAPITALS PLEASE

Surname..

Address..

....

....Postcode ....

Send this whole page to:
UK: The Reader Service, FREEPOST CN81, Croydon, CR9 3WZ
EIRE: The Reader Service, PO Box 4546, Kilcock, County Kildare (stamp required)

Offer not valid to current Reader Service subscribers to this series. We reserve the right to refuse an application and applicants must be aged 18 years or over. Only one application per household. Terms and prices subject to change without notice. Offer expires 31st August 2000. As a result of this application, you may receive further offers from Harlequin Mills & Boon Limited and other carefully selected companies. If you would prefer not to share in this opportunity please write to The Data Manager at the address above.

Mills & Boon is a registered trademark owned by Harlequin Mills & Boon Limited.
Enchanted is being used as a trademark.

MILLS & BOON®

*M*akes Mother's Day special

For Mother's Day this year, why not spoil yourself with a gift from Mills & Boon®.

Enjoy three romance novels by three of your favourite authors and a FREE silver effect picture frame for only £6.99.

Pack includes:

Presents...™
One Night With His Wife by Lynne Graham

Enchanted™
The Faithful Bride by Rebecca Winters

TEMPTATION®
Everything About Him by Rita Clay Estrada

Available from 18th February